STONE-HEARTED ALPHA

COLD-BLOODED ALPHA, BOOK 3

EVE BALE

CONTENTS

About Stone-Hearted Alpha — v

Chapter 1 — 1
Chapter 2 — 13
Chapter 3 — 28
Chapter 4 — 38
Chapter 5 — 51
Chapter 6 — 60
Chapter 7 — 66
Chapter 8 — 75
Chapter 9 — 85
Chapter 10 — 98
Chapter 11 — 111
Chapter 12 — 118
Chapter 13 — 126
Chapter 14 — 139
Chapter 15 — 146
Chapter 16 — 155
Chapter 17 — 166
Chapter 18 — 173
Chapter 19 — 178
Chapter 20 — 192
Chapter 21 — 205
Chapter 22 — 222
Epilogue — 230

Also by Eve Bale — 235
Thank you — 237

This is a work of fiction. Names, characters, places, and incidents either are the product of the author's imagination or are used fictitiously. Any resemblance to actual persons, living or dead, events, or locales is entirely coincidental.

Stone-Hearted Alpha
Cold-Blooded Alpha Series, Book 3
Copyright © 2021 by Eve Bale

Cover designed by Starlight Covers

ALL RIGHTS RESERVED.
No part of this book may be reproduced or used in any manner without written permission of the copyright owner except for the use of quotations in a book review.

www.evebale.com

ABOUT STONE-HEARTED ALPHA

Lost...

All I want is to outrun the ghosts that haunt me…

But instead, my nightmares chase me into the arms of an alpha who has my wolf eager for a closer sniff, and desire overwhelming my wary human side.

I never count on a night of passion leading to a mate I don't want, don't need, and have every intention of rejecting. A shifter determined to drag me back to a place I swore I'd never return.

A place where old enemies have resurfaced.

He's unmovable. Stone by name. Stone by nature.

Will Jeremy, the stone-hearted alpha, be the biggest mistake of my life or the best?

Due to adult language, violence, and steamy scenes this book is recommended for 18+

CHAPTER ONE

"You can't hide in there forever, Savannah," a male voice, low with amusement, drawls from the room next door.

In response, I close my eyes and rest my head against the closet wall, hoping, praying, wishing this is all a dream. That none of this is happening, because none of it seems real. None of it *feels* real.

How can it be that less than an hour ago, I was in my cabin figuring out what to eat for dinner? Right up until I picked up Jeremy Stone's scent and knew he was here in Hardin, and why he'd come.

For me.

Somehow, he's tracked me down, and instead of cornering me in my cabin as I expected, he headed toward the Lake, where Dayne and the others would finish the pack run.

I've never shifted to wolf and run so fast in my life.

Even then, it still wasn't fast enough to intercept Jeremy before he got to Dayne and revealed my secret.

Or rather, before he forced me to reveal I had a mate.

Even knowing this is no dream, it's not enough to stop me from hoping that when I next open my eyes I'll be back in my cabin in the woods, waking from one of the many nightmares which haunt me.

But of course, when I open my eyes and gaze around me to take in the mostly empty closet, I can still scent the shifter in the room next door.

Not just any shifter, Savannah. Mate. Your *mate. The guy you ran away from in the middle of the night.*

"I'm not hiding," I mutter as I shove my legs into a pair of blue skinny jeans.

I assumed that I'd left them behind in Dawley when the pack and I went to rescue Talis from her evil Uncle Glynn, but all these months they were here.

Since we left Hardin in a hurry, I'm not surprised to find several tops tucked in the corner, as well as boots I have no memory of bringing with me from my cabin.

I hate it here. I hate Jeremy for forcing me back here.

Well, maybe not *forcing* me.

I guess we could've gone to my cabin to get some privacy from the pack. Only I couldn't stand the thought of him invading my private space. My sanctuary.

Better we're here than there, I try to convince myself.

It doesn't help when all I feel is a rising tension that never abates until I'm back in my cabin.

Still, it's a relief to find I've got clothes here since the idea of facing Jeremy naked is enough to make me not want to come out again. Ever.

We shifters aren't usually hung up about nakedness, both ours and others. But remembering the intensity of Jeremy's gaze on me when I announced to the pack that he was my mate, made me aware of my body in a way I've never been before.

I slip into a white embroidered peasant top, but I don't go anywhere.

"Well, I'd call it hiding. Or did you need help in there?" Jeremy calls out in his husky voice.

Sexy. The other word you're forgetting, Savannah, is sexy.

This time when I close my eyes, it isn't to pretend I'm back in my cabin, but to focus on my breathing. Namely, slowing it down.

He's right. I *am* hiding, which isn't the best idea when it's only a matter of time before Dayne, Talis, and the rest of the pack tire of waiting for us to come down.

Dayne especially is going to want to know why I've been hiding Jeremy from him.

As my alpha, adopted brother, and the last remaining member of my family, he'll be the most pissed, and feel the most betrayed that I didn't tell him.

I should have. Then maybe none of this would be happening.

Dayne won't just want an explanation. He'll *demand* one, and I'd better get my story straight with Jeremy or the fight I broke up by the lake will be on again, and this time no one will be able to stop it.

I suck in a deep breath and quietly release it, taking a moment to wipe all expression off my face before I force myself to retreat from my hiding place.

The first thing I notice when I step into the bedroom is that he hasn't dressed in the sweatpants Talis loaned him.

Distantly, I'm aware of them, neatly folded at the foot of the bed. Yet that's not the most exciting thing in the room.

He is.

He hasn't managed to fit all six-foot-two of his tanned, lean muscled form on the bed, and his feet are hanging off the edge. Only, I'm not looking at his feet.

Nope. My eyes are focused on something else.

Something that has arousal spiking and my mouth going dry.

Something that looks pleased to see me.

I know because it's standing to attention.

"Hey there," Jeremy murmurs.

My eyes shoot up to his face and find him eyeing me with not a small amount of interest stirring in his whiskey brown eyes as his gaze slides down my body.

With his arms pillowed under his head, all I'm

thinking about is how the last time I saw him stretched out like that, both of us were naked and I was straddling him.

No matter how much I tell myself to think of something else. To not go there, I learn that saying and doing are two different things.

"You dressed," Jeremy says, sounding disappointed as his gaze settles on my breasts.

Even if I couldn't see where he's looking, I'm convinced I'd feel the heat of his gaze because it's like a physical touch, caressing me.

I plaster a severe expression on my face, hoping it's enough to hide the direction of my thoughts, and that Jeremy doesn't notice how his close attention has made my nipples hard in record time. "And you haven't done anything but lie there."

The sharpening of his gaze tells me Jeremy is more observant than I want him to be.

"I was waiting for you." His focus never shifts from my pebbled nipples.

"You think you could look at my face for a minute?" I say through gritted teeth.

"Why? You're a model, I'd have thought you'd be used to people spending more time looking at your body."

For a second, I stare at him, unable to summon a coherent response.

His words are so beyond anything I could have

expected him—or anyone—to say that all I can do is just gape at him, even as my anger wakes up.

I'm mated to a pig.

I shake my head, trying to wrestle my dawning fury back inside me. We don't have time for this. *I* don't have time for this.

It doesn't matter. After I've convinced Dayne not to kill Jeremy, he won't be my problem for much longer. It'll be a couple of days at a push. Any longer and I'll kill him.

This is temporary, I tell myself. *Temporary*.

"Look, whatever," I say breezily.

When he suddenly raises his gaze, I can't hide my relief that he's *finally* stopped staring at my breasts.

Jeremy's gaze turns thoughtful, and then the smile is back in his eyes, even if it doesn't touch his mouth.

And what a mouth it is.

I remember him trailing kisses along my jaw and down my neck, and when arousal once again stirs, I shove it right back in the hole I've been keeping it.

He's a pig, Savannah. Remember that he's a pig, and an untrustworthy one. Remember what he did to you?

"I see," he murmurs.

I blink. "You see what?"

With no warning, Jeremy rises from the bed in a graceful move that has his pecs, abs, and delts rippling.

Despite my intention to keep my gaze on his face, I find it slipping down, down, and fixing between his legs.

He's still rock hard.

"Sounds like you've got a plan, sweet."

I wrench my gaze back to his face as he stalks over to me.

He crosses over to me as if he isn't completely naked, as if he owns the room and everything in it. Me included.

If my agent, Paulo, saw him, he'd sign him in a fucking heartbeat.

"Don't call me that," I snap.

I have no idea where the ridiculous name came from, only I didn't mind it when he growled it in my ear when we were strangers in a Chicago bar.

Not sweetheart or sweetcheeks or sweetie pie. Just sweet.

But now? I'm finding it's just another thing that sets my teeth on edge.

"Tell me this plan of yours, sweet."

I tense the closer he approaches as I stand with my back to the wall, but I don't move. I'm not intimidated by him in the least. Sure, he's a six-foot-two alpha who at twenty-eight is in the prime of his life. But he doesn't scare me.

At five-eight, he's not *that* much taller than me, and even if he were, I still wouldn't go anywhere.

"I don't know what you mean," I say as he stops directly in front of me. A whole lot closer than I want him to be.

Up close, it's impossible to ignore his scent. He's an

intriguing mix of wild forest, warm vanilla, and an underlying scent that's him and him alone.

My wolf growls her approval at my choice of mate.

Shut it, you. You're just as much of a traitor as he is.

My wolf makes her displeasure known by gently raking her claws against me. Not hard enough to hurt, but enough to make me snarl, one she follows up with another low growl.

With a flick of her tail, she settles down now that she's got the last word in.

I don't provoke her anymore, since it'll get me nowhere. While the wolf and human side of me are usually in harmony about all things, Jeremy Stone proves the exception. We won't agree, so I'd just be fighting my wolf side for no reason.

She's alpha. I'm alpha. Neither of us backs down easy.

"To deal with me," Jeremy says, as he rests one hand on the wall over my head while he lifts the other to my face.

My hand snaps out and locks around his wrist as I narrow my eyes. "No touching."

This time the smile in his eyes makes it to his mouth.

He leans closer. Close enough for me to feel the hot brand of his cock nudging against my lower belly. "You sure about that, sweet? I have distinct memories of you screaming at me never to stop."

Oh my God. This guy is going to kill me.

"Hey, you guys all right in there?" Talis calls out from somewhere downstairs.

"No," I shout.

At the same time Jeremy shouts, "Yes."

We stare at each other, and there's a tense silence from downstairs.

"I meant yes. Yes, is what I meant," I shout, a little desperately when Jeremy leans even more of his weight against me.

Jeremy lowers his mouth to my ear. "I remember you screaming that as well. Hmm, what was it, again? Yes, Jeremy, give me—"

There's no hiding the scent of my arousal as his words triggers our sex-filled nights in Chicago. "Please, just… stop. Okay?" I beg him. "We can't talk about this here."

"Savannah!" Dayne calls, sounding like he's started up the stairs.

None of this is going the way I expected it to. And as time goes on, I can see it getting even more out of control if I don't reign Jeremy in.

"We'll be right down," I shout back, and keeping my head down, attempt to slip around him.

Only there's no getting around him. He has me trapped.

I eye his wrist and wish I hadn't bothered to grab it. Him touching me with his hands would've been better than him leaning his naked body against me like this.

"You should get packed," he says, surprising me

when I was fully expecting this to turn into a badly time quickie.

A quickie, I might add, that I would have done everything in my power to stop.

My wolf snorts at my firm mental declaration.

I would have stopped it.

There's more amusement from her, but this time she stays silent.

I lean my head back against the wall to get further away from Jeremy. "Packed?"

"I need to go talk to the guy downstairs."

"My alpha?"

"Your *former* alpha."

I open my mouth to correct him, only he raises an eyebrow a shade darker than his tousled chestnut hair, which brushes against his nape.

He's right. Jeremy is an alpha, which means as his mate I become the Luna of his pack. If he had a pack that is. For the time being, at least, I tell myself.

"Former alpha," I repeat.

He holds my gaze as if he knows what I'm thinking, but he doesn't comment.

Instead, Jeremy steps back, and I release his wrist since he's moving away.

His gaze takes in the mostly empty room. "You don't have much."

"This isn't my room." I keep my eyes on him.

It's a nice room. Airy and painted lilac with dark-stained wooden furniture, but Jeremy is right, there's nothing much in it. It's got the feel of a guest room that's been rarely used.

Although he raises his eyebrow, as if he's waiting for an explanation, I don't offer him one.

"I thought you said you had to talk to Dayne?" I ask, folding my arms over my chest when he continues to observe me in silence.

Alphas. They're all the same.

What was it Talis called Dayne?

Yeah, alpha dick. And it would be no stretch of the imagination to assume Jeremy Stone is as bad—or worse—than Dayne.

"I did," he murmurs as he stares at me some more, an air of expectation in his silence.

"Well then," I offer brusquely as I cross over to the bedroom door and jerk it open, "best not keep him waiting."

I have a second to wonder if it might not be the best idea to antagonize a shifter—an alpha shifter—I barely know like this before he's stalking toward me, his eyes unreadable, and his focus so intent on me, it's a wonder he doesn't walk into the bed.

When he reaches me, he stops and stares down into my eyes without blinking. "Hmmm," he murmurs, reaching a hand to my face.

I force myself not to grab him as I did before. "What?"

"Just surprised." His eyes continue to drill into mine.

"By what?" With him standing this close to me, I have a sudden urge to roll around in his scent the way I would crispy leaves in fall, or freshly fallen snow.

"I hadn't thought you were an alpha, is all."

I freeze.

All this time I've been meeting his eyes, staring him down. Not lowering my gaze, the way any other wolf would.

Shit.

"I don't… I don't know—" Belatedly I shift my gaze away, but of course it's much too late for that.

Jeremy's fingers tighten on my chin so I can't break our gazes.

For a second, he lets his wolf out and I see the wildness in him. His eyes lighten to golden-hazel, and I know it's his wolf studying me.

He smiles. But it's a smile full of hungry anticipation. Like a wolf before a hunt.

"Should make things interesting," he says, and then he releases his hold on me and walks out.

He shouldn't know I'm an alpha. It's something I made damn sure to keep hidden from him in Chicago, but now it looks like the cat's out of the bag.

Since the alpha trait is more common in male shifters than in females, no alpha is going to let his female alpha mate walk away without a fight. Which means getting away from Jeremy Stone just dialled up close to impossible.

Fuck.

CHAPTER TWO

"He's hot," Talis murmurs as we start down the front steps of the main house.

I doubt I have long to pack and say goodbye to everyone before Dayne kills Jeremy for invading his territory.

The only thing that calmed him down was Talis and Regan's offer to come to my cabin and help me pack. It also means Talis isn't anywhere near Jeremy, which I guess was the reason Dayne practically shoved her out of the door.

With Talis and Regan helping me, it means I can get packed sooner, and Jeremy and I can be on the road before ten.

As it's late already, it's going to mean us staying in a motel on the way to wherever we're going, which sounds like fun. Not.

I shoot a glance toward the office window where

Dayne and Jeremy are having their discussion. "I wouldn't let Dayne hear you say that, what with the baby making him crazy and all," I warn her.

Talis places a hand over her rounded belly and grimaces. "I know right. Just think what he'll be like when Squirt's actually running around. Will he even let me pick her up?"

"I'm still not convinced it's a girl," Regan, who's been quiet up to now, offers.

Talis glares at her. "Don't you dare even suggest such a thing. God, if I'm wrong Dayne will *never* let me live it down."

"You don't want a boy?" I ask as I lead the way through the forest toward my cabin, relieved for the time being no one is asking me questions I'm still trying to formulate answers to.

Talis' expression softens, and her large brown eyes warm. "I didn't say that," she murmurs. "I think a mini Dayne would be the cutest thing ever."

Every time I speak with Talis, I'm always surprised by how much energy and spirit she has, considering everything she went through. She's all alpha. Protective, fearless, and strong.

That kid is going to know so much love.

"He *was* a cute kid," Regan concedes.

"Yeah," I add. Dayne was blond-haired and blue-eyed, and very cute. Even if he was just as demanding as he is now. "But bossy. So, good luck raising an alpha kid like Dayne."

It provokes the terror I was hoping to inspire, and Talis looks so horrified that I can't help but laugh.

"So, Jeremy Stone," Regan prompts.

When I turn to her, I find her waggling her eyebrows suggestively. "Give us the dirty. The low down, deep down, *dirty*. And hold nothing back. The nastier, the better."

"Can you stop doing that, please?" I say coolly. I imagine I'm meeting a new client and eager to prove I'm the experienced model they're looking for.

Regan snorts. "That won't work on me, you know. Not after I caught you burying your poop in the sandbox that time."

My face is flaming hot in less than a second.

Talis' laughter explodes out of her. *"What!"* she gasps.

"That wasn't me. I told you I was—"

Regan raises an eyebrow. "Somehow, I doubt it was Dayne. I didn't believe you then, and I don't believe you now. So, Jeremy. Spill. *Now*."

Talis hunches over, tears streaming down her cheeks. "No, no. Let's go back to the sandbox and the poop. I don't even care about Jeremy now."

It's so mortifying, I can't help but shoot a glance back at the house and hope that we were far enough away that Jeremy didn't hear Regan.

"Well, tough, I do." Regan's narrowed hazel-green eyes warn me she's not about to back down anytime soon. "But I can tell you later since

Savannah will only keep interrupting to deny it, anyway."

Sighing heavily, I wait for Talis to stop dying of laughter as we approach my cabin, a small log structure in the forest.

It was an older, abandoned building built by the alpha before Owen, but it was Dayne who spent a lot of time and money making it—and a couple of others nestled in the forest—liveable.

"Don't you have work early tomorrow?" I ask, leading the way into the one-room cabin.

"Day off. So… Jeremy Stone." Regan goes straight to the refrigerator in the tiny kitchen and pulls out bottles of water for us.

I drag my big work suitcase out from under my bed and dump it on top.

When Regan is like this, it's impossible to shake her off the scent. There'll be no convincing her to drop it until I tell her *something* about Jeremy.

Once Regan's handed out the water and settled on the couch alongside Talis, I open my suitcase and start talking, "I met him in a bar in Chicago."

"When? 'Cause I'm sure you weren't rocking that bite when we were in Dawley," Talis says, opening her bottle. "One of us would've seen it."

"No. It wasn't then. It was when we'd got back, and I had that work trip in New York."

Or at least I told them I had a work trip. That's not to say I didn't go to New York. I did, but to meet with my agent to talk about a big Paris job I wasn't—and I'm still not—ready to tell anyone about.

"Anyway," I keep talking when it looks like Regan's about to ask me a question, "the trip isn't important. After, I decided to take a couple of days for myself in a place I'd never been before."

"But... *Chicago?*" Talis wrinkles her brow. A glance in her direction proves she isn't buying this. "You go to Paris, Monaco, and London. Why *Chicago?*"

I grab a handful of clothes at random from the dresser and start folding. "That's for work. And it's not like I'm ever really visiting anywhere interesting. More often than not, I'm in my hotel, or working, or grabbing takeout to bring back to my room. It's not all that exciting."

"But then why do you do it?" Talis asks. "I'm sure you don't even have to work at all. The pack does well enough."

She's right.

Things are good *now*. But they weren't always.

When Dayne took over as alpha, pack finances weren't great. If anyone less determined than Dayne had taken charge, I doubt the pack would have had the main house now.

None of us realized how bad things were until Dayne found all the letters Owen had been hiding. He'd mortgaged the pack land and the main house to the hilt, and it was only a matter of time before he lost everything.

Things were so bad that Dayne pretty much worked from dawn to dusk. First, to uncover all the things Owen had been hiding. Then he was down at the bank, trying to convince the bank not to foreclose because of all the missed payments.

Since Dayne had always taken an interest in finance and investing, he took what little money was left and kept investing it over and over.

It took years. And in those years, he barely slept. And somehow, in the middle of it, he lost even more sleep trying to track Talis down.

I still can't believe he did, and that he had time to check up on me as well.

Things are a little different now he's mated.

Dayne still works longer than he should, but he takes more time off to spend with Talis, and all the time he put into learning about investments and pulling the pack out of the red and into the black has more than paid off.

Now that he has Talis to help, we all see him more than we did before.

I'm sure if I didn't want to, I wouldn't have to work at all, but not working would mean staying here in Hardin permanently, and I can't do that.

So, I push myself to keep on doing it, not because I have any real desire to be a model, but it gives me an excuse to be away from Hardin.

All because I can't bring myself to tell Dayne I don't

want to be here anymore, and that I haven't for years now.

I shrug. "It's what I know."

When Talis' brow creases and she looks poised to push, I smile gently. "I thought you wanted to know about Jeremy?"

"I do," she admits, though her frown remains. "But not at the cost of talking about something important, like you."

And that's when I know how far she's come.

In four months, she's become the Luna this pack didn't know we needed. She's grown so much, which only serves to remind me how little I have, and how stagnant my life has been for years.

"I don't, but thanks, Luna," I tell her.

Although she flushes, and waves her hand at me with a hurried, "No need to call me that," it's hard to miss how much she likes the title.

"So." I resume folding. "Chicago was just a short break. It was close. It was the next flight leaving New York, and I thought, why not?"

"And you met your mate. It must be fate." Regan slumps back on the couch with a happy sigh, her long honey-brown hair fanning behind her.

I think back to the dark and dingy bar I met Jeremy Stone and my reckless act.

Fated mates? Not a chance.

If Regan ever learned how we met, she'd either

laugh herself silly or refuse to believe I was telling the truth.

The idea of the serious, prefers-the-quiet-of-living-in-a-cabin-in-the-woods-with-books-for-company Savannah Blackshaw going prowling for a one-night stand is impossible to imagine.

Even now *I* struggle to believe it happened.

"Well, we met in a bar, and we hit it off."

I told him I wanted a one-night stand, no strings attached. He bought me a drink and slipped his hand under my skirt. I came that first time in a dark corner booth with the people all around us none the wiser.

"We talked a little, and we realized there were some things we had in common."

Namely that I wanted to fuck him, and he wanted to fuck me.

"So, we decided to go someplace else and get to know each other a little better."

We fucked again in the back of his car. I came twice then.

"It wasn't long before we realized we'd formed a real connection with each other in a short time. It seemed impossible, but it was true."

He took me back to his place, and we had sex again in the elevator going up, against his front door before he got it open, and then on the floor just inside.

At that point, I passed out or fell asleep. I'm still not sure which, but when I woke up, we were in his bed, and he had his mouth between my legs.

"I don't know if you can call that fate. But it was intense."

For nearly forty-eight hours we never left his bed unless it was to use the bathroom or get food. We barely spoke a word to each other. Just fucked like bunnies, and no matter how many times we did, I always wanted more, and he never seemed to get enough of me either.

"So, that's about it, really."

As Jeremy and I lay there on the second night, which should only have been one, I'd started thinking about when I'd have my next one-night stand because clearly, I'd been missing out. I figured if this is what it was like, I needed to start spending a little less time in my cabin and a little more time hitting the bars.

Sometime between us talking, and my making plans to leave, we had sex again. And that was when he bit me.

Mated us together, in other words.

I finish folding the last of the clothes I'm taking with me and turn to the bookcase but pause when I find Talis and Regan staring at me with their faces expressionless.

Regan sucks in a breath. "That's the biggest load of bullshit that I—"

"—Regan!" Dayne's voice from the doorway cuts her off, and Regan closes her mouth, even though I can see she still wants to argue.

I peer around Dayne, but there's no sign of Jeremy filling the doorway.

"He went to get his car," Dayne says, stepping into the cabin and closing the door behind him.

"Oh." I wait for the inevitable explosion or the flurry of questions because Dayne knows me well enough to know a story when he's heard one.

And although he gazes at me seriously, he doesn't look as pissed as he did earlier.

I can't help but wonder what they were talking about, and why their conversation didn't take near as long as I thought it would.

"He'll be back for you shortly," Dayne adds.

He stops to press a kiss on Talis' hair as he passes her on the couch.

It's so sweet to see how instinctive, how natural, it is for him to kiss her, and for her to kiss him back.

They're in harmony with each other.

Sometimes, I see it when they're walking together. They adjust their pace and it's like they don't even realize they're doing it.

Part of me wonders if it's the mate bond that makes them so good at reading each other, or if it's love.

"Oh, okay," I say, and resume packing.

Since I alternate between jeans and the occasional sundress, there's little in the way of clothes I'm attached to. Not like some girls I've worked with who would've happily stabbed another girl in the back to get the better outfits.

But like I said, I never became a model because I like the idea of travel, or fashion, or a need to be famous.

Those were never my reasons.

"And you're happy about leaving?" Dayne asks as I head to the bookcase and take a lot more care in choosing out my favorite books.

With the shelves full to bursting, I know I can't take everything, but I'll take a good handful. Maybe twenty for now, and I can always come back and grab more in a couple of weeks.

"Sure, I'm mated to Jeremy. I know we couldn't stay. You'd want to challenge him, and he would want to challenge you. So, I have to leave."

"But are you *happy*?" Dayne's stare is probing. "Because if you're not, I can kill him, and then there'd be no question of you leaving."

I can't help but smile as I place the books in the suitcase before I cross over to the couch and pull him into a hug. "I love you for the offer, and I appreciate it, but there's no need for you to kill Jeremy."

I can get myself out of this on my own.

"You know you've always got a place here, right?" Dayne's arms are a familiar warmth around me, and I feel my eyes fill with tears.

Family.

He's the only family I have left in the world, and it doesn't matter that I'm adopted, because it doesn't feel like it. He's never treated me anything less than a full sister.

"I know," I say with a voice husky with tears. "But I have to leave now."

And not just because of Jeremy.

I know that if I don't leave, and soon, I'll fall so deep into myself that my misery, guilt, depression, and anxiety will swallow me whole and I'll never be the same anymore.

Dayne squeezes me hard and edges back to press a kiss on my brow. "I know," he says in a way that has me searching his eyes because it sounds like he really does know.

But he's got his unreadable expression on. The one that had everyone convinced for years he was the cold-blooded alpha when nothing could be further from the truth.

I blink my tears away and force a smile on my face. "I know this is all very last minute, my leaving like this."

"Come back next weekend," Regan says, rising from the couch. "We'll go for a run and have the BBQ we were supposed to have tonight."

In response to her words, Talis' stomach rumbles. Loudly.

We all turn to find her glowering, her hand over her belly as if to muffle the sound. "What? I can't be the only one hungry?"

Dayne slips an arm around her waist and tucks her under his shoulder. "Nope. Just you, piggy." He gives her head a hard kiss, and when I see the violence in her eyes, I wonder how Dayne can sleep with both eyes closed.

"You're playing a dangerous game riling a pregnant woman like that," I warn him.

Although I'm an alpha, I'm nowhere near as hot-tempered as Talis can be. She's like a lit firework. There have been more times than I can remember that my packmates have come to my cabin to wait out one of her explosions.

Once Luka joked that Dayne only built her a cabin so he could get some peace in the main house.

Luka spent the next week hiding out in my cabin. She got him eventually, though he refuses to say what she did. Whatever it was, it must've been bad, because he hasn't taunted her since.

Dayne's grin comes out of nowhere. "I know, exciting, isn't it?"

"Alphas," Talis grumbles, giving me a loaded look of warning, "just you wait."

"Which is why you won't catch me making that mistake," Regan says smugly, ignoring mine and Talis' glare. "So, do you know where you're settling?"

Since I have no plans of sticking with Jeremy for too long, it doesn't matter, so I shrug. "I don't know. We haven't talked about it."

And it's the truth. We haven't. We haven't talked

about anything. Not even this mating. I foresee hours of fun in his car when he arrives.

"Since Jeremy doesn't have a pack of his own, and Dawley's in need of one, he suggested checking it out."

At Dayne's words, a chill spreads over me, and for a second I remember the cold eyes filled with malice glinting at me from Dawley National Forest.

The same stare chased me back into the main house when I caught sight of the unknown shifter outside my cabin.

But Abel's dead. Dyne killed him. I *know* this. But it still isn't enough to silence my fears.

I consider telling Dayne I don't want to go with Jeremy, that this is all a terrible mistake. But then I imagine what would happen if I told him I didn't want to go.

Dayne would fight Jeremy, and Jeremy had tracked me down here intending to claim me.

There's no way he's going to walk away without a fight.

A big one.

I'm sure Dayne could defend himself—win, probably. But what if he doesn't? What if Jeremy hurts Dayne badly, and he dies? What happens to Talis and their baby then?

"Savannah, are you all right?" I jump, startled, at Talis' hand on my arm. I have no memory of her moving closer to me, but she's close enough I should have noticed.

There's worry deep in her eyes. Worry for me.

I can't let anything happen to Dayne. I can't let anything threaten her new happiness, a thing she's fought so hard for.

And anyway, I have no intention of staying with Jeremy for long. Just long enough for my backup plan to kick in, and then I can invent some story about how things didn't work out when I come back to visit Hardin.

It'll only be a couple of days.

But first I'd need to have built a new life for myself, otherwise everyone will just expect me to move back to my cabin and everything will go right back to the way it was before. Something I can't let happen.

"I'm fine," I reassure her.

"You look pale," Regan says.

I plaster a smile on my face. "I'm okay, promise. Come on, let's finish up here and go feed Talis before she kills Dayne," I joke.

I head back to the bookcase to grab more books, but the moment I've turned my back, my smile slides away.

I'm going back to Dawley, a place I swore I'd never return, and a place which has done nothing but reawakened my nightmares.

How the hell am I supposed to hide them from my new mate?

CHAPTER THREE

"So, you wanna tell me why you ran?"

I don't take my eyes from the view outside my window. "Not really."

"That wasn't a question."

Well, it sounded like one.

I consider arguing back, or lying, and open my mouth.

"The truth."

I turn to find his eyes on me instead of on the road. "What makes you think I'd tell you anything else?" I ask in a meek voice.

He raises an eyebrow and turns his gaze back to the mostly empty highway.

The roads have been so quiet since I said my tearful goodbyes to my pack—my former pack—in Hardin and climbed into Jeremy's black truck.

We're making good time, like really good time. Which means I have less time to prepare for my return to Dawley.

Since it doesn't look like we're going to be stopping at a motel anytime soon, and I doubt Jeremy's going to let me dodge too many of his questions, I give him the truth.

Well... I decide to tell him a more palatable version of it. Something which isn't going to start a fight.

"I didn't like Chicago."

"So, you wanted to return to your cabin in the woods, is that it?"

I narrow my eyes at him. "Who told you...?"

"I pay attention," he replies, giving nothing away.

If that's what he wants to believe, who am I to convince him otherwise, so I shrug. "Sure."

As my gaze returns to the dark landscape outside my window, I can't help but wonder why I was so desperate to return to a place that over the years has left me feeling more and more stifled.

It could be Dayne and Talis, and wanting to return to my pack, but I know that's not it.

Even now, it makes no sense to me. Not when I ran to Chicago to get away from Hardin because it felt like I couldn't breathe anymore.

"But that's not it," Jeremy says, proving to be some kind of mind reader since he doesn't even pose his words as a question.

I let out a heavy sigh. "You're a guy I met in a grungy bar. I think I can be forgiven for not wanting to tell you my life story."

"If that's all I was, I guess," he says. "But since I'm not…"

The entitlement I hear in his voice has me turning from the Rockies, a dark shape set far in the distance, to face him. "I hope you're not about to insist that as my mate, you now have rights over me," I say, keeping my voice mild.

A brief smile touches his lips, though he keeps his eyes on the road. "You're my mate. That means I have rights over you no one else does. It means…" He turns to eye me. "…that you're mine."

"You bit me without my permission," I tell him, letting him hear the sharpness of my anger. "I did not want any of this. All I was looking for was a night of sex with a stranger that led nowhere. And instead, I got you. I got a mate. A mate I didn't want."

"So, that's why you ran then?"

"Yes," I say, struggling to understand how he doesn't get it. "When instead I should have rejected you first."

His jaw locks. "I wouldn't try that if I were you."

I arch an eyebrow. "Why? Will you wreck the car to stop me?"

"I'll do whatever it takes."

I stare at his profile, not knowing if he's joking or if he's being serious.

Since I'm in no hurry to burn in a fireball at the side of the road, I let him have this round. I turn away and go back to staring out of the window. "Well, no need to drive us into a tree. I won't do it now."

"Which means you intend to do it later?" His words are as mild as mine, but there's a simmering heat beneath the surface. He's pissed. More than pissed. And he's driving.

"If you don't let me go, then yes."

"I note you didn't say any of this back in Hardin, back when you had the protection of your former alpha."

"I can take care of myself. I don't need his protection." My words come out more sharply than I intended, and I mentally shout at myself to rein myself in.

I need to remain calm, cool, focused. It's going to be the only way to deal with someone like Jeremy.

"So, you were looking for a reason to leave then?"

Briefly, I close my eyes. The man is dangerous. He is too observant by far, and he doesn't even need to be looking in my face to read me.

I try for casual since cool and collected seems to be out of touch. At least for the moment. "Look. None of that has anything to do with you. All I wanted was a night of sex, nothing permanent."

"I see," he says. "So, any guy would've done as long as you got your itch scratched, is that it?"

There's something in his tone that warns me to be wary, even though his face is devoid of expression.

Then I remember I didn't want any of this, and if Jeremy's feelings get hurt because he pushed something on me I didn't want, then that's on him, not me.

"Well, if I'm being honest, yes. Actually. Any guy would have been fine."

I wait for the inevitable explosion. But when he merely nods as if we're talking about the weather, I can't help but feel a touch... disappointed with his reaction.

"But then you bit me," I say when he doesn't respond.

His hands tighten around the wheel. "You were going to leave."

"I left anyway. Couldn't you just... I don't know, say you wanted me to stay?"

Jeremy snorts. "Would you have stayed?"

I don't have to think about it for a second. "No. No, I wouldn't. But that still doesn't give you the right to tie us together when you knew full well I was only looking for a fling. I was very clear about that in the bar."

"I'm an alpha, Savannah. When we see what we want, we take it."

For a second, I'm distracted because the way he says my name is so sexy that I'm reminded of him growling it in my ear when he climaxed inside me.

I make a sound of frustration at my inability to

control my hormones, and because Jeremy still isn't getting it. "I'm a person. Not a thing. You can't just—"

"Then you shouldn't have tangled with an alpha."

I open my mouth to complain.

"Your former alpha, Dayne." He shoots me a side look. "I see he's mated. From our first meeting, I get he's possessive of her and would've acted that same way even if she hadn't been pregnant. Are you telling me he didn't go after her hard once he knew she was his?"

I start to deny it.

The thing is, I can't because I know he's right. I want to ask why he's so convinced I'm his, but I don't. I just sit there, stewing in my frustration and my anger.

Once Dayne returned from the meeting of alphas that he attended in place of Owen, he became obsessed with finding the girl he saw crying there. Talis. He focused all his efforts, all his energy on tracking her down because she was his.

When I asked him how he knew, he said he just did. Not because Talis was his fated mate, but something inside him refused to let him walk away from her.

Fated mates are rare. So rare that I don't know anyone who's found there's. But it's a soul mate thing. Dayne's parents once told us our heart, our soul would just know when we'd met the other half of us.

Since I can't remember the last time I peered into my heart, I wouldn't know I'd even met mine. The only thing I have in my heart is the pain of everything I've lost. I don't need to be reminded of it, so I don't turn my gaze inward. Not anymore.

But fated mates are an impossible dream few shifters can ever hope of having.

"How did you even track me down?" I ask instead.

On the third morning of mine and Jeremy's planned one-night stand, I slipped out early and headed straight to the airport. I struggle to understand how he tracked me down to a tiny town in Colorado, which is pretty much in the middle of nowhere.

Finding Hardin, to put it mildly, is not easy if you've never been there before.

"I was motivated, and I'm ruthless about going after what I want."

"Well, it doesn't matter," I reply, brushing his words aside.

"Because you've planned something out?"

I remember him saying almost the same words back in Hardin. "What makes you think I have?"

"Maybe because the last time you told me it doesn't matter and brushed me aside like that, it was after I'd bitten you, and the next morning I found you gone."

Right. Well. He might have a point then.

Clearly, I need to rethink what I say around him. "If you're afraid some shifter won't want you because I've rejected you, then I have no problem with you rejecting me. You can do it in public if you want, that way no one will think it was me throwing you away because I didn't want you."

There's a long pause before Jeremy speaks, "So, you'd prefer it if I threw you away instead? In public? Humiliated you? Ensured that every male shifter would look at you and wonder what it was you'd done that your mate had publicly rejected you, and likely ensured you remained alone forever?"

I'm not prepared for the sharp sting of his words. Because yes, while I accepted it on a mental level, to hear him tell it back to me… hurts. *A lot.*

So, I shrug like it doesn't bother me. "Yes. It's not like I've ever been interested in settling down, anyway. I'll be fine."

"You don't strike me as the type of girl happy to live a life of no-strings sex, and commitment-less short-term flings. And trust me, I know. I've met more than a few."

Unexpected jealousy flares at the thought of all the women who've come before me, but like the pain of his rejecting me, I shrug as if it doesn't matter. "It's my life."

"Right. So, you want me to reject you and then you, what…?"

"Get on with the rest of my life." Since I have no idea what that looks like, I figure the less I say, the better.

"And relationship-wise? What if you get lonely?"

"There are guys in bars all over. I doubt I'd have to look very hard to find a guy interested in no-strings sex."

As soon as the words come out of my mouth, I realize I shouldn't have said it.

It's hard to know what it is about Jeremy that changes. It isn't his expression, or that he says anything. I just get the sense I've made a big mistake.

The silence that follows my words is the longest so far, and I'm struggling to figure out what to say when he nods again.

"I see. Anything else you want to get off your chest?" he asks, his voice mild.

I gaze at him warily. "Not really."

He nods again and focuses on the road ahead. "You sure about that?"

"Crystal."

"So, we just sit here for the next however many hours in silence then?"

Although I met Jeremy in a dingy bar, I'm getting the sense he's the high-maintenance sort. "It's not my job to entertain you. Nothing is stopping you from turning the radio on, you know?" I snap.

Then I lean away from him because I've let him provoke me into losing my temper, and alphas have never taken too kindly to someone snapping at them.

I still have the recent memory of Talis ready to kill me when I snapped at her in Hardin about charging after Dayne to rescue him from Glynn Merrick. And this alpha, Jeremy Stone, doesn't seem the sort to let something like that go.

Jeremy stretches a hand in my direction, making me flinch since I'm expecting him to lash out at me.

But after a pause, he moves his hand. Not to hurt me, but to switch on the radio.

Slowly, he returns his hand to the steering wheel.

I examine his profile a little while longer, then when nothing happens, I turn my face to the window as classic rock fills the tense silence in the car.

CHAPTER FOUR

I'm dozing off with my head against the window when Jeremy speaks, startling me. "Stay here, I'll book us a room."

Before I can do more than turn to him, he's out of the truck and slamming the door shut before striding off toward a dimly lit motel reception.

Part of me is appreciating his ass in his blue jeans, but a larger part of me is thinking about what he just said.

A room.

I could run after him to check, but I think I'd know what the answer would be.

We're going to be spending the night together. Presumably sharing a bed, since something tells me he's not going to be booking us two rooms.

As I lean my head against the seat-rest, I consider booking a room since it isn't like I don't have money of my own. But it isn't hard to see how that's going to work out. Badly.

After telling him he's replaceable with just about any guy in a bar, I can't imagine that's going to work out well for me.

When my phone vibrates, I reach for my bag and pull it out.

Even though it's late, nearly three, I know who it is before I look. My agent, Paulo, who's in the middle of trying to set up a new job for me.

This is the job that will give me the perfect excuse to stay away from Hardin for a while. A good long while.

Most girls would kill for the opportunity to be based in Paris for six months with one of the biggest designers in the world, working as the in-house model to prepare for them launching their next season's line at Paris Fashion Week.

The job comes with everything, an apartment, insanely generous pay, working with designers that will launch any model to supermodel status.

Yet, instead of telling anyone that I want to leave Hardin because there are too many ghosts, I push for a job that means I won't have to admit it. And this dream job will do that.

His text message is brief. *Nothing solid yet gorgeous. But soon.*

I try not to feel too disappointed as I tap out a quick reply. *No worries. Speak soon.*

After I've sent the message, I sit there, staring down at my phone.

It was too much to hope, I guess, that Paulo would text me to say everything was good to go, and I'd disappear to Paris where Jeremy wouldn't find me, and eventually, he'd give up and I'd be free.

But that didn't stop you from hoping anyway, did it?

When there's a knock on the passenger window, I jerk in surprise to find Jeremy stood beside the truck.

I shove my phone in my bag, and he pulls the door open, giving me not nearly enough space for me to step out. Once again, putting us closer together than I'd like.

"Anything interesting?" he asks, his eyes going to my bag.

I edge around him. "Not really. Which is our room?"

Only, I don't get far. Jeremy's hand snaps around my wrist, halting me.

I make a sound of frustration. "Is this you being jealous, because really, I'm too tired and hungry to deal with it right now. So, can we please just get inside?"

A line forms between his brow, but he doesn't let go of me. "Why didn't you say you were hungry, I would've stopped."

I pull at my arm, so he knows I want him to let go.

He doesn't. At this point, I think I'd be surprised if he did anything I wanted him to.

"Jeremy, can we please just—"

"Get in the truck. I saw a diner still open a few miles back."

Thinking he's being ridiculous, I huff and start complaining. Only I stop when I see the genuine concern in his eyes.

"It's not your job to feed me," I murmur instead.

Jeremy lifts a hand to my face and traces his fingers along my jaw. "Yes," he says, distinctly, his eyes on my mouth. "It is."

Arousal stirs in my belly at the heat in his eyes. I swallow. "Well, there's no need. I'm fine."

He steps closer. "You said you were hungry," he says, his voice deepening.

My mouth goes dry at the thought of him kissing me. "I'm more tired than anything else. Really, I'm just ready for bed."

Seconds after the words leave my mouth, I realize talking about bed with Jeremy gazing at me with heat in his eyes was not my best idea.

The sexual tension ramps up even higher as Jeremy bends his head lower, and I wait with bated breath for his lips to touch mine.

Only, I feel eyes on me, and my gaze shifts over his shoulder to find a guy behind the counter, standing with a candy bar in his mouth, his eyes locked on me.

"Stop. A guy is staring at us," I murmur.

"And here I thought you didn't have a problem with me touching you in public," Jeremy says gruffly, lifting his head.

I turn to face him as a blush spills over my cheeks. Once again, his eyes are laughing, though it doesn't reach his mouth.

"You don't have to keep bringing it up all the time, you know." I place my hands on his chest. At the warmth I feel radiating from him, a heat I'd forgotten, I pause.

But when I realize what I'm doing, I do what I'd intended on in the first place and shove. "Back up."

Jeremy doesn't move an inch. "Or what?"

I gaze up at him. He's too big and likely too strong for me to move.

"Considering you've claimed to be concerned with feeding me, keeping me pinned to your truck when you know I'm exhausted goes against this idea it's your job to care for me."

A slow smile stretches across his lips at my mild rebuke. "Feisty," he says. "I like it."

With that, Jeremy turns and rounds the truck to the bed.

"I wasn't trying to be *feisty*," I tell him, letting out a silent sigh of relief.

"I know. What the hell do you have in here? Rocks?" Although he's grumbling as he lifts my suitcase out of the back, there's nothing on his face to suggest he's struggling.

"Books. And there's no need to get it out if we're only here for one night. I have a change of clothes in here." I hold up my bulging purse, where I shoved a t-shirt, panties, and a few of my toiletries while I was packing back in Hardin, anticipating we'd be staying overnight in a motel.

"I didn't know models knew how to read," Jeremy says as he returns my suitcase and removes a small black duffel from beside it. His clothes, I guess.

Since I know he's just saying that to provoke a reaction from me, I choose not to comment on it. "So, which is our room?"

He slams the tail gate shut and eyes me for a couple of seconds in silence before starting for the line of motel rooms.

On the way, he stops to glare at the guy still staring from behind the counter, and who soon disappears from view. "I thought you'd have a problem with us sharing."

"Which I guess is why you did it, huh? Well, I'm not going to make it easy for you." I wait beside him as he unlocks the motel room and shoves it open before indicating I step in first.

"Does that mean you're not going to bite?" Jeremy asks, following me in and closing the door behind him.

I take a second to scan the simple motel room with the one bed I was expecting, little in the way of furniture and a closed door I'm guessing leads to the bathroom.

My eyes go to his throat, and I bite my lower lip. "Is that what you were hoping? For me to bite?"

At his silence, I shift my gaze to his face, and his

eyes are dark with heat. I know he's remembering the time he pinned me against the wall, and I felt the urge to bite him, right on his throat, and he just about lost his mind. I don't think I've ever come so hard in my life.

His bag hits the floor, and he moves forward a step. "I'm open to suggestions," he growls.

I force myself to turn away. "Sorry, but no thanks. I won't be long in the bathroom."

Although I wait for him to tackle me to the ground, or stop me, he does neither, and so I go to the bathroom and close the door behind me so I can brush my teeth and get myself ready for bed.

Minutes later, when I step out and find Jeremy laying naked on the bed, I freeze.

"Come to bed, Savannah."

I don't move. It was one thing knowing I'd be sharing a bed with Jeremy, but the idea of actually doing it is something else.

"Are you afraid you'll like it?" The amusement in his voice has me gritting my teeth.

Yes.

"No. I just know you won't keep your hands to yourself, and I'd like to sleep."

"I have no intention of getting in the way of you and your beauty sleep."

He's mocking me about being a model. Again. But I refuse to let him get to me because the moment I snap back, he'll just keep on.

"Whatever," I mutter, and cross over to the bed, doing all I can to ignore his nakedness stretched out in front of me.

"Can you move over, please?" I ask when he doesn't move.

Like in Hardin, Jeremy folds his hands under his head and gazes up at me. "No."

Which means I'm going to have to climb over him. That's what he's hinting at, since there's no other way of reaching the space he's left on the other side of the bed.

"You're being really immature. You *do* realize that, right?"

"Is that what I'm doing?"

We stare at each other for several seconds, and I realize he's not going to budge, which means I'll have to. If I want to get any sleep tonight, that is.

I put my knee to the edge of the bed, intending to crawl over him as fast as possible.

Only, the moment I've thrown one leg over his hips and I'm astride him, Jeremy's casual pose falls away, and his hands lock around my hips, halting me.

"I have no complaints if you wanted to stay there," he murmurs, his gaze going to my mouth.

At the intimate press of him nestled between my legs, for a moment I don't speak, so I shake my head instead. I realize I've made a mistake. I should've just slept on the floor or found some other to get around him.

"No? You sure about that?"

My body is screaming out for his, and there's no doubt he can smell my arousal with me wearing nothing more than a pair of lace panties and a t-shirt.

The problem isn't that my body wants his, but that the rest of me doesn't.

"I'm sure," I say, fighting the need to rock against him.

"So, you're telling me that if I were to strip these panties off you, I wouldn't find you so wet I wouldn't even need to touch you to get you ready for me first? That I wouldn't just slide right to the hilt? Is that what you're saying?"

Moisture floods my panties in response to his words because it's all too easy to remember him doing just that, filling me so utterly, I nearly cried at how good it felt.

Jeremy inhales and at his low growl, I can't stop myself from shifting on him as I fight back the urge to tear my panties away and sink down on him.

"Savannah?" One of Jeremy's hands glides up my back and bunches in my hair, tilting my head up so we're eye to eye. "Tell me that isn't what you want."

I'm desperate to just give in because the sex between us was incredible. But this won't be no strings attached sex. I'll be having sex with my mate.

A mate I never wanted.

And every time we do, we'll be getting closer. I'll be letting the mate bond develop to the point that walking away won't be an option anymore because he'll be in my head, as much as I'll be in his.

It'll be permanent, no rejection possible. Not ever.

The knowledge of what would happen if I let something happen between us again is enough to harden my heart, if not cool my body's response to his.

"I don't want this," I tell him, looking him in the eye. "And I don't want you."

He gazes up at me in silence.

Although my words come dangerously close to my outright rejecting his claim, he doesn't say a word.

When I stare down into Jeremy's eyes, something warns me that rejecting him would only be one part of it.

He's already tracked me down once before. Would he let me walk away, even after I'd rejected him? And what would happen with the mate bond?

I'd always have the bite on my throat. But what would happen if he refused to let me go? And if he bit me again? Would that trigger a new mate bond?

Since I've never heard of anything like that happening before, I wonder if that isn't a future I'm looking at now.

As I tense, eyeing Jeremy's expressionless face, I'm not expecting him to pull his hands away. "Go to sleep, Savannah."

Without another word, I slide off Jeremy and turn to face the wall, grabbing for the sheets to cover myself.

"And lose the shirt."

At his words, I freeze, then I glare at the wall. "No."

"You don't wear a shirt to bed from now on. Out of the kindness of my heart, I'll let you keep the panties. But no shirt."

Out of the kindness of his heart?

"But I—"

"Or I'll take the panties when I tear that shirt from you."

Which means we'll both be naked.

I squeeze my eyes shut at the memory of his naked body draped over mine, clamping my legs together as I hope he doesn't notice.

"Not a chance."

His words have me jerking my head to his side, heart-pounding, terrified he's read my thoughts.

I find him gazing up at the ceiling with a smile curving his lips. "Are you worried I'm reading your mind, sweet?" He shifts his gaze to me, and there's still heat in them.

"No." I search his eyes as I try to convince myself he just got lucky.

It took Dayne and Talis weeks before their mating bond strengthened enough for them to be able to read each other. There's no way mine and Jeremy's would snap into place while thousands of miles separated us.

When he raises his eyebrow, I jerk my gaze away

and go back to staring at the wall. For about two seconds, that is.

"The shirt."

I grit my teeth. "I don't see why—"

"I guess that means the panties are coming off." I feel him shift, and panic races through me.

I hurry to sit up and slip the shirt over my head, leaving it at the bottom of the bed so I won't need to crawl over Jeremy in just my panties the next morning.

Then I tug the sheets up over me and go back to staring at the wall.

When Jeremy doesn't move, I relax, thinking he won't.

But, just as I close my eyes, he turns over and tugs the sheets down to my waist before curving his body flush against mine.

My eyes fly open, and I tense.

Jeremy wraps an arm tight around my waist. "Go to sleep," he murmurs, pressing a kiss to my mate bite that has me biting off a moan.

"I can't. Between you and the sheets, I'm too hot."

I realize I shouldn't have said anything when Jeremy peels the rest of the sheets off my body, leaving him as the only thing covering me.

"There you go," he says. "Now go to sleep."

"That isn't what I meant."

I don't even know why I'm arguing since nothing about the arm Jeremy has clamped around my waist gives me any indication he's intending on moving it.

"Hmm." Although he sounds half asleep already, I'm not convinced, especially when I attempt to wriggle away, and in response, his arm tightens.

I growl in frustration and feel his lips curve into a smile against my shoulder.

Minutes pass. Then an hour, and my eyelids get heavier and heavier until finally they close as I relax into the overly soft bed.

Despite the wall of heat at my back, and the hard ridge of Jeremy's cock tucked against my ass, tiredness overwhelms my resistance and I fall asleep.

CHAPTER FIVE

"*D*id you know you talk in your sleep?"

At Jeremy's question, I jerk my gaze away from the early morning views outside my window and turn to face him.

He's wearing a fresh white t-shirt, though he's still in the same blue jeans he was wearing the night before.

"Do I?" I ask, trying to sound as if I'm not terrified by the thought of what I might have said.

In the same casual voice, he taps his fingers on the wheel and shoots me a glance. "You seemed to be having a nightmare."

Oh shit.

I'm surprised he didn't mention it when we woke early that morning.

I remember waking to find Jeremy studying me with an inscrutable look on his face, and I had the sense he'd been awake for a while.

He must have been thinking about telling me then.

Only, he didn't. He asked if I wanted to use the bathroom first, and since I had no intention of climbing over him again, I told him he could.

But he didn't move. Not at first. He just studied me some more. When his eyes dipped to my bare breasts and I yanked the sheet up to cover myself, he shook his head with a faint smile on his lips and went to use the bathroom.

"Really?" I ask as I try to hide my tension.

There's another pointed glance. "A bad one."

I give him my most convincing smile, the one that fools everyone but my former pack. "I guess most girls in my position would have a nightmare or two."

"I take it you're placing the blame at my door?"

Since I have no memory of my nightmare or of anything I might've said, I shrug. But inside I'm shaking because this is what I was afraid of, the nightmares.

It was the main reason I went to New York and then Chicago. To escape them.

"It wasn't as bad in Chicago."

Although Jeremy's tone is casual, I'm horrified. "In Chicago? You didn't say I had a nightmare then."

"It was one night. When you didn't mention it the next morning, I guessed you didn't want to talk about it, or you didn't remember it."

Ah. So that was what he was waiting for this morning. For me to tell him about my nightmare.

I decide to go on the attack since I have no intention of opening up to Jeremy. About anything. Ever. "You still didn't hear me mentioning it, but that hasn't stopped you from bringing it up now."

He takes the next exit off the highway, and as we're still hours away from Dawley, I'm guessing we're stopping for breakfast. "This is twice now. Which suggests a pattern."

"No, it doesn't."

"Yes. It does."

I don't say anymore as he parks up in front of a Denny's in a mostly empty parking lot, but he doesn't get out. Just turns the engine off and turns to face me.

For several seconds, we do nothing but stare at each other in silence.

"Are you waiting for me to get out?" I ask since there's no way we're going to be talking about the other thing.

"No. I'm waiting for you to tell me about this nightmare of yours and whether it was what you were running from."

"I wasn't running from anything." I turn to shove the passenger door open, only Jeremy's hand closes tight around my wrist, like a manacle. Unbreakable.

Growling in exasperation, I spin around, ready to snap at him. But the intensity of his gaze has me forgetting what I was about to say. It's like he's trying to peer into my soul, that's how hard he stares deep into my eyes.

"You'll forgive me if I don't believe you, Savannah. I saw the look in your eyes when you wandered into that bar in a part of town you had no right to be. I know desperation when I see it."

As I'm still trying to process his words, and how... absolutely *right* his guess is, Jeremy releases me to grab his keys before climbing out of the truck.

"Come on. Since you can't feed yourself, looks like it's up to me to make sure you get fed."

He slams his door shut, and I take a second to work on my deep breathing exercises since keeping a tight rein on my anger around Jeremy Stone isn't easy. And then I force myself to get out.

Going by the lingering glances our server, a teenage girl with long brown hair and hazel eyes, keeps giving me, it doesn't take me long to guess she recognizes me.

When she repeated Jeremy's order back to him wrong twice, he didn't snarl as I'd expected him to, just quietly corrected her before turning to me with a raised eyebrow.

A scan of the plastic-covered menu reveals nothing on it that I'm interested in. Although I know I should eat, thinking about my returning nightmares and wondering what Jeremy might've heard me say is all I can think about.

"I don't mean to sound weird, but are you Savannah Shaw?" the server asks in a timid voice.

I lift my head from my sticky plastic menu and smile at her. "There's nothing weird about it, and yeah, I am." I grab a handful of my unwashed and no doubt greasy hair that I didn't want to wash because my long blonde hair takes forever to dry. "Please don't tell anyone."

She sighs. "You look amazing. I wish I looked like that in the morning. God, if you had any idea what it was like for the rest of us."

I frown at her, ignoring the weight of Jeremy's gaze I can feel on me. "I *am* the rest of you." I scan her name badge. "Lyra?"

She shrugs.

"Northern Lights is an old favorite. You're so lucky, I'd have killed for my name to be Lyra."

Lyra's eyes widen. "You've read Philip Pullman? That's who my parents named me after."

"Again, super lucky. And I love Philip Pullman. I think I'll always prefer the books though, no matter how many movies they keep making. What about you, book or film?"

Lyra doesn't even pause. "Book. Definitely book." Then she chews her lower lip. "I, uh, I have a magazine in the back. You're actually in it, but I didn't know you were in it until after I bought it, and then I saw you. God, that sounds kind of stalkery... Uh, do you mind signing it for me?"

I smile brightly at her. "Not stalkery at all. Go grab your magazine. I still need a couple of minutes to decide what I want."

She takes off at a near run, and I give Jeremy a quick peek.

He's sat back in his seat with his arms folded across his chest, observing me.

"What?"

"Shaw?" he asks.

"It was to stop stalkers and weirdos from tracking me down," I say, giving him a pointed stare so he knows I'm talking about him.

He shakes his head with a wry smile, but before he can comment, Lyra returns clutching a copy of Cosmopolitan and a sharpie.

I put my menu to one side and take the pen and the magazine she's holding open to a spread I did in Paris a few months ago.

In the picture, I'm leaning off a balcony with the Eiffel Tower in the distance, wearing an elaborately beaded dress, six-inch heels, and my long blonde hair is a frizzy cascade going down my back.

"Oh, I remember this one," I say, as I scrawl Lyra's name at the top. "I was so terrified I'd fall off the balcony that they had to keep re-shooting it and re-doing my make-up because I was sweating it all off."

Lyra sucks in a sharp breath. "They actually made you do it? I thought it was all effects."

I shake my head. "No. They made me do it. I don't think the supermodels do though, but the rest of us…"

"And have you met them? What are they like?"

I consider her question as I scrawl my message. Once I've finished, I close the magazine and return it. "Not perfect. Because that doesn't exist… for anyone. We're all like everyone else, no matter what this tells you." I gently press the magazine into her hands. "So, it's good genes. That and filters. Lots and lots of filters."

Lyra laughs and takes the magazine before her gaze returns to my menu. "Are you ready to order?"

"I can't decide what I want. How about you choose something for me, Lyra?"

Before I've finished speaking, she's shaking her head. "Oh, I can't… not—"

"Please, whatever you choose will be great. Regardless of what you've heard, we models do eat. Usually at night, under the sheets, with a flashlight. But we do it."

My joke draws another laugh out of her, and she nods. "Okay. If you're sure."

I nod back. "I'm sure."

After Lyra heads to the back to place our orders, Jeremy clears his throat and I turn to find out what he wants.

"Back in Chicago, when you told me you were a model, you didn't say that you were famous," he says, with no hint of expression on his face.

I shrug. "I do okay."

"Well enough to be in magazines even I've heard of,

and for strangers to recognize you and want your autograph."

"One teenage girl recognized me," I correct him.

Jeremy nods toward the kitchen without taking his eyes off me. "Want to try saying that again?"

When I turn to see what he's talking about, I find three men staring back at me from the kitchen, mouths hanging open.

I guess Lyra told them who I was.

I raise my hand and finger wave. They return my wave, and the three faces disappear from the hatch.

"It doesn't happen often." I turn back to him with a frown. "Anyway, I thought you knew that. Isn't that how you tracked me down?"

Before he can answer, Lyra returns with our coffee and leaves again after telling us our food will be ready in about twenty minutes. "It looks like it happens a lot," Jeremy says after she's left, ignoring my question.

I shrug since there isn't much I can say to that.

Yeah, I sometimes get recognized, but not as often as Jeremy seems to think it does. Maybe if I lived somewhere less isolated than Hardin, it would've happened more, but I doubt it.

I take a sip of my coffee. While it's not the best I've ever had, it's nowhere near the worst either, so I sip a little more.

"You were good with her. Maternal," Jeremy says suddenly, sounding thoughtful.

My cup slips out of my hand and crashing to the table, sending coffee spraying everywhere.

I jerk to my feet and grab for some napkins, my eyes on the table and deliberately *not* on Jeremy.

Between Lyra returning to clean the table and my rushing to the bathroom to mop up the worst of the spillage on my top, our previous conversation is forgotten.

Jeremy's words well and truly destroy the last of my appetite. Still, I force myself to eat every last mouthful of the breakfast Lyra picked out for me, keeping my head down, and saying not another word to Jeremy as he silently focuses on his meal.

CHAPTER SIX

The rest of the drive continues mostly in silence. While Jeremy listens to a breakfast show on the radio and then switches over to a local rock station when the show ends, I lose myself in memories of the past as I stare out of the window.

After Jeremy paid for our breakfast and we left the diner, I sat in a tense silence waiting for him to ask why I dropped my coffee.

While I know I could get away with saying it slipped out of my hand, I have no excuse if he asks why it happened right after he said I was maternal.

But Jeremy surprises me by not pushing, which makes me think that he knows I'll lie if he asks me, or I'll refuse to talk about it.

Whatever the reason, when he doesn't demand any answers, I can't help but feel relieved.

Right up until we reach Dawley in the early afternoon, and he pulls up in front of a house I never, ever wanted to see again.

He turns the engine off, and although I can feel his eyes on me, I don't move.

"Savannah?"

I stare up at the three-story white-wood house with a wraparound front porch because it's better than taking in the Dawley National Forest that sits alongside it.

"Yeah."

"Something wrong?"

Why can't I stop staring up at the house? And why of all the homes in Dawley does the one we're staying in have to be this one? Surely, there are a million other homes available to rent.

"No," I murmur, distracted.

"I can smell your fear."

I tear my gaze away from the house and turn to face him.

He has his keys in his hands, and his door is open as if he were about to get out but noticed I hadn't moved.

The smile I'm so used to seeing in his whiskey-colored eyes is notably missing. He looks serious, and I know it's because he's right, I've filled the truck with the scent of my fear.

Since I have no idea what to say, I say nothing.

"You're not speaking," he says, his eyes never leaving mine.

Although Jeremy looks far too sober to crack some

stupid comment about me being a model, the thought of telling him about my fear isn't an option.

I couldn't speak even if I wanted to because I'm trapped in the past.

The wolf with the terrifying eyes—Abel, Talis said his name was—is dead. I saw his body with my own eyes after we buried the bodies of the Merrick pack.

Those that didn't run, that is.

But even knowing that he's gone, the memory of him, the terror of seeing him staring at me from the Dawley National Forest, refuses to loosen its grip on me.

"Savannah?" For the first time, I'm hearing the concern in Jeremy's voice, as his eyes focus on me with an intensity I don't want.

It takes serious effort to bury my fear and force an airy smile on my face as I turn away. "I thought you were going to kiss me, that's all."

Without waiting for a response, I shove my truck door open and step out.

"Still thinking about me kissing you?"

I can't stop myself from jumping when Jeremy appears beside me at the window of the master bedroom, and the room he's told us we're sleeping in.

It's the room Dayne and Talis stayed in before, and even though the elegantly furnished room has been deep cleaned after we left it, my shifter nose still catches their scent.

I blink at him in confusion as I struggle to work out what he's talking about, and when he raises his eyebrow, I realize what he means. The scent of my fear is back.

"Uh, yeah."

He stares at me a long moment, then he shifts his gaze to the window. "You see something?" he asks, his eyes searching the forest.

"No. Are we going out to eat, or doing a grocery run?" I cross over to my suitcase, which Jeremy has carried from the bed and left on top of the bed.

Something in his eyes tells me he didn't miss my retreat. "Not fussed. You want to eat out?"

Once I've unzipped my suitcase and pulled out a handful of books, I scan the room for a bookcase since I know a house this fancy must have one. "I don't mind."

Bingo.

Spotting a half-filled shelf in the corner of the room, I grab another handful of books and head for it. I might *just* have enough room to squeeze them all on.

"I'm surprised you're not kicking up a fuss about us sharing a room."

When I turn to Jeremy and find him leaning against the window, his eyes tracking my progress, I shrug. "Would it make a difference?"

"I thought you had some plan to get out of this."

I return to the suitcase for more books. "If I did, I certainly wouldn't tell you what it is, now would I?"

"Whatever it is, you might as well drop it. It's a waste of your time thinking you can escape."

A smile forms at his words, and I grab the last of my books. *"Escape.* Interesting word. Does that mean you have me trapped?"

Since I didn't hear him move, when hands grip my hips and turn to press my back against the wall, I jerk my eyes to his face in surprise.

"Something like that," he murmurs, leaning so close that I wonder if he isn't about to kiss me. And like an idiot, I do nothing but stand there, waiting for him to do it. "And Savannah?"

His eyes are on my mouth. I can feel the heat of his gaze, and my lips tingle with awareness. "Mmmm."

He bends even closer, and my eyes go to his lips. "You can't lie worth a damn. So next time, don't."

My eyes snap up to his, and as if that was what he was waiting for, he drops his hands from my hips and turns to walk away.

I panic at the thought of him leaving me alone in this house. "Where are you going?" My question comes out sharper than I intended.

Jeremy pauses and turns to me. "I need to make some calls. You need me?"

To hold my hand while I unpack? No thanks.

I force a casual shrug. "No. Just wondered how long

before we go…" My voice trails off at the hardness in his eyes.

"What did I just say?" In a moment he's all alpha, expecting instant obedience.

I gather he's picked up on my lie.

"I don't know. I wasn't listening. Was it important?" I arch an eyebrow as I wait to see how he's going to react.

"Get unpacked," he says, turning away. "We'll go out to eat in an hour."

The moment I hear his footsteps descending the stairs, I sink to the edge of the bed and drop my face into my shaking hands.

How the hell am I supposed to deal with being back here? And with us sharing a room, how long before Jeremy clocks in on that something is wrong and forces me to talk about it?

Alphas aren't exactly known for their patience.

And just what exactly am I supposed to tell him when the nightmares start back up again?

CHAPTER SEVEN

I'm sitting on the bench at the back of the house, sipping from a mug of herbal tea on a warm summer night.

It's so peaceful that I'm about to put my mug on the floor and lay on my side to see if I can't sleep out here. But just before I do, I have a sudden awareness that I'm no longer alone.

Someone is watching me.

I scan the dense dark forest in front of me, my heart pounding with rising fear.

I tell myself not to be silly since it can't be Abel because Dayne killed him. I'm on my own, and at worst, it's nothing more than a wild animal.

Even knowing this, it doesn't stop me from rising and abandoning my mug to head back inside.

At no point do I take my eyes from the forest

because I know—I'm absolutely certain—that the second I do, someone is going to rush at me.

I fumble for the door handle and jerk it open before backing inside. Only to stop when I bump into something.

I let the back door slam shut as I turn to see what it is, thinking I dropped something on the floor before I came out.

Bodies covered in blood, eyes staring at me from where they lie, leave me frozen in horror.

And in the corner of the room, I spot a hunched-over figure covered in blood. It's a man, and I don't have to see his face to know who he is. Owen. The alpha before Dayne.

As if he feels my gaze on him, he slowly rises.

I back up because the outside has to be better than in here. I have to get out. Now.

I manage two steps before an icy hand, wet with blood, seizes my ankle and yanks. Hard. Making me scream.

I fall.

My back slaps against the floor, winding me. Then the hand starts dragging me, and I open my mouth.

Another scream comes pouring out as I struggle and fight, even though I know there's no escape. There's only one person who can save me, and he's not here. I'm all alone.

I scream louder, fighting with everything I am.

"Savannah!"

I struggle to free myself, but I can't. I'm pinned down and he's so strong.

"Savannah!"

Why can't I get loose? How can he be this strong?

"Savannah, stop it. It's me, It's Jeremy."

The name penetrates my mind, but I shake my head as I fight to get free.

"Open your eyes. It's just a nightmare. You've had a nightmare."

What he's saying doesn't make sense. I was only unpacking a few minutes ago. It was daylight—afternoon—far too early for me to be asleep.

No. That isn't right.

I finished unpacking. I'm sure of it. I remember dragging the suitcase in the closet when I was done.

I remember Jeremy taking me out for lunch, then we stopped at a grocery store to grab some food for dinner, where we argued non-stop all the way around. About *everything*.

I lost count of how many times I planned on running Jeremy over with the shopping cart, but somehow, I managed to restrain myself. Only because I realized it wouldn't do near enough damage.

And I remember people asking how long we'd been married, which made me flush with embarrassment and Jeremy grin down at me.

All of that was hours ago.

I know this because I made up a quick spinach salad

with steaks for dinner. I read while Jeremy made more calls, and then I went to bed.

Which means he's right. I never went out to the back. Not once.

I was having a nightmare. A bad one.

I open my eyes and realize why I found it impossible to get free. Jeremy is half lying over me, with the bedside lamp on illuminating the otherwise darkened bedroom.

While Jeremy is naked, the only thing I'm wearing is my panties, and I'm covered in a cold sweat that smells of terror.

"Are you with me now?" he asks, releasing his hold on one wrist he's pinned to the pillow.

That's when I notice the deep scratch on his cheek.

My eyes widen. "Oh, God. I scratched you."

Since I have no memory of unsheathing my claws, it must've been while I was fighting to get free of him—or Owen in my nightmare.

For me to lose control like that is beyond dangerous, and the thought of what else could've happened hits me.

I could have cut his throat and not even known it. I could have killed Jeremy.

"Small price to pay," he says, amusement dancing in his eyes.

I stare up at him, my breathing unsteady, filled with horror at the thought of waking up beside Jeremy's dead body.

My nightmares have sometimes been so bad that Dayne heard me screaming from the main house and came running to the cabin.

They've been so bad there were times no one could reach me. It was as if my nightmares had me trapped and I had to find my own way out.

But Jeremy got me out.

"Savannah, what—"

I use his shoulders to pull myself up before fusing my lips against his and slamming my eyes shut.

For one second, Jeremy stills against me, and then, with a low groan, he dips his head and kisses me back.

I sink into it, not letting myself think of anything but the solid weight of Jeremy's body pressing mine into the bed as I wind my arms and legs around him.

Jeremy deepens the kiss, and I moan into his mouth at how good it feels as I run my hands over his back, delving into his muscles and exploring every inch of skin I can get my hands on.

When he grabs at my panties and starts tugging them down, my body goes taut with anticipation because I know soon he'll be inside me again.

Jeremy's next groan is full of frustration, and despite my desperate attempt at stopping him, he breaks our kiss and raises his head.

His eyes burn with need, and he's fighting to catch his breath as much as I am. "Savannah…" His voice is a low growl, and I can't help but want him even more.

"Why did you stop? I want you." I rub myself against him and feel him hardening against my belly.

He closes his eyes and forces a deep breath out before opening his eyes to pin me with a dark stare. "No. You don't want to tell me what this was about."

I shake my head. "No, you just don't want me."

Jeremy presses his cock into the vee of my thighs, making me moan. "Since we both know that isn't true, what terrified you?"

I tear my gaze from his. "I don't want to talk about it."

Jeremy bends closer, making it impossible for me to avoid his eyes. "And why do I get the feeling it's what had you running before?"

Once again, I curse his ability to read me.

"I don't know what you mean," I say, trying to steady my breathing.

"It's the look in your eyes. I've seen it before."

"Well, that didn't stop you from fucking me before," I snap. "So, I don't see why you're suddenly concerned now."

The heavy silence that follows my words is almost painful, and the fury lighting his eyes makes me wonder if I've gone too far.

For a second, regret wavers in my mind because he didn't deserve that. Not after he pulled me from a nightmare.

"I see," he says, in a deceptively mild voice.

Deceptive because his eyes warn me that he's anything but calm right now.

"You see what exactly?" I ask because I'm scared that I've said too much, that I've shown him too much.

"You think I took advantage of you."

Is that what I'm saying?

When I don't respond, the fury builds in Jeremy's eyes.

"You think my desire to fuck you was more important than anything you might need. So, you think I took advantage of you."

I realize that's pretty much what I'm accusing him of, and he's right to be pissed because I'm making it his fault, as if I didn't go looking for some way to hide from my nightmares.

"That isn't what I'm—"

When Jeremy suddenly pulls away from me, a feeling close to panic rises.

"You know what, I think I need a drink." He moves to the edge of the bed and prepares to stand.

"You're the only one that's ever made me forget," I blurt.

Jeremy stops moving, just sits with his back to me, on the edge of the bed. "Forget what?"

I pull the sheets up over my chest and stare up at the ceiling, willing my tears away. "The pain. The guilt. All of it. So, if anything, I think I took advantage of you." My words end in a whisper as I continue to stare at the ceiling.

"What would you need to feel guilty about?"

I shake my head.

"And this pain?"

Although I feel him shifting to look at me, I don't turn to meet his gaze. "I can't…" I shake my head again because even if I wanted to, there's no pulling the words free from where they've lain buried deep inside me for years. "I can't."

I'm expecting him to push me for answers, but when he slips back into bed and moves me so my head is resting on his chest, I blink in surprise.

"Sleep now," he says. "We'll talk in the morning." He reaches out and flicks the lamp off.

I lie there in the dark, swimming in confusion. "What if I don't want to talk in the morning?"

Jeremy wraps his arms tighter around me. "Then we won't."

I curl an arm around his waist as I fight back a yawn. "You know, you're a lot nicer at night than during the day," I tell him.

With my face against his chest, I feel his silent laughter. "So are you, sweet. Go to sleep."

I grumble since I know that isn't true, but I slowly let sleep overcome me.

Just before I drift off, I have a sudden realization I might fall right back into the same nightmare.

I jerk awake and struggle to get up. "No. No, I don't want to."

I sound like a petulant child. I know it the instant

the words leave my mouth, but Jeremy doesn't laugh or make fun of me.

He presses a hard kiss on my brow and holds me even tighter. "I have you, Savannah. I won't let go. Sleep."

And even knowing that's the very opposite of what I want, that his words shouldn't fill me with this much relief, somehow they just… do.

My eyes drift closed, and I sink against Jeremy, comforted beyond measure at the feel of him holding me close.

CHAPTER EIGHT

"So..." Jeremy drawls.

I lift my head from my phone and meet Jeremy's eyes over the rim of my coffee cup early the next morning.

We're in the spacious white marble and stainless-steel kitchen, sitting opposite each other on the island instead of in the more formal dining room.

It felt too much like we'd be having a romantic breakfast when Jeremy asked whether I wanted to sit in there, so I told him I preferred the kitchen.

After my nightmare, I'm still warming myself up to the idea of breakfast, although Jeremy demolished a couple of scrambled egg and sausage burritos with what looked like half a bottle of sriracha.

He gazes back at me expectantly, his cup sitting on the table in front of him.

"So?" I repeat coolly when he says nothing else.

The next several seconds pass in silence, and when I don't fill it, Jeremy's lips quirk in a quick grin. "I'm heading to the old Merrick house. I want to check out the land before making an offer on it."

My stomach cramps at the thought of going with him, much less having to live in the house filled with Talis' pain and fear.

"Oh, okay. Well, I'm heading into town to—"

"You're coming with me," Jeremy interrupts.

I stare at him. "Unfortunately, I can't. I'm sure it's only a matter of days before I leave on assignment, so I need to prepare for it."

Jeremy sits back in his seat, his face is expressionless. "And this assignment? Where and how long?"

I shrug. Best start laying the groundwork for my leaving now, I figure. "London, or maybe Paris, I'm not sure yet. I'm still waiting to hear from my agent. And it could be anything from two weeks to two months. It depends on what the client wants."

I go back to sipping my coffee and scanning my phone, hoping he isn't observant enough to have picked up my barefaced lie.

Yes, alphas can pick up lies, but I'm not one of his pack that he can sniff the truth from. I may be a trauma-ridden alpha with more ghosts and nightmares than strength, but I *am* an alpha.

"We leave in twenty minutes. You want to eat before we go?"

I choke on my coffee when it goes down the wrong

way and cough to clear my throat before I speak. "Excuse me?"

"You heard me."

I stare at him. "But I just said—"

"I know what you said."

I return my cup and phone to the table. Now it's my turn to sit back in my seat, face expressionless, a fury rising deep inside me. "So, what is this, then? You attempting to railroad me into doing what you want? Do you think I'm going to just let you shove aside my needs? My career?"

Jeremy reaches for his cup and raises it to his lips. I shudder at the sight of him drinking black coffee with nothing in it. No milk. No sugar. Nothing. Who *does* that?

No one, that's who, Savannah. No one.

His lips twitch at my reaction. "No. This is you stepping into your new role."

"As Luna of what pack? There is no pack in Dawley, and even if there was—" I stop before I can finish my sentence, but at Jeremy's raised eyebrow, it isn't hard for him to figure out what I was about to say.

"You wouldn't want to be Luna, anyway?"

I force my eyes from his. Not because I'm backing down, but because if I don't, I see myself picking up my coffee cup and hurling it in his face. Something in his eyes is driving me to it.

"I'd rather not have that discussion," I tell him instead, reaching for my phone.

Only just before I can, Jeremy beats me to it.

I stare open-mouthed as I watch my phone disappear into his pants pocket. "Give me back my phone," I snap, feeling my wolf waking up. "What if my agent calls?"

I'm slow to anger, and it takes a lot to push me into a rage, but this alpha is managing to do it in record time.

Jeremy downs the rest of his coffee and rises with his cup. "After we see the Merrick land, I might think about giving it back to you. *If* you behave, that is."

For a second, I'm so enraged, I lose the ability to speak. So, I let him see my wolf in my eyes. And his response? A smile flashes across his face.

"Hi, darlin'. It's about time we were introduced." His eyes flash and it's his wolf gazing back at me.

I shift my gaze to my half drank coffee on the table.

My fingers itch with the need to pick it up and fling it at his head.

"Thinking about making me wear it, sweet?" Jeremy asks as I hear him rinsing his cup out at the sink.

"You know what, I was wrong last night. You aren't nice at night, you're a dick. An alpha dick. Morning, noon and night."

"That isn't a nice thing to say," he says, sounding as if it's the funniest thing he's ever heard.

With my control hanging by a thread, I rise from my seat, and without glancing in his direction even once, because I know full well what will happen when I do, I turn and walk out of the kitchen.

"Twenty minutes, Savannah," Jeremy says when I get to the door, just before I can step out. "Or I'll come and get you, and sweet? You're not going to want me to do that." There's steel beneath the pleasant tone, and I curl my fingers into tight fists that I picture smashing into his face.

I continue walking away, head held high and at an easy pace.

After I point-blank refused to go into the house, Jeremy went in to have a look around while I wait for him at the foot of the porch stairs.

Even from here, I can smell Talis' terror, as well as the blood from the Merrick-Blackshaw fight several months ago. Well, not that *I* did much fighting, not with Gavin, one of the best fighters in my former pack standing guard over me.

Pretty much all I saw of the fight was Gavin's ass, or his snarling face when he swung around every time I tried to help.

It's a place filled with so much anger and pain and death that I doubt any shifter would ever willingly choose to live here. Not one sane, that is.

This place needs to be knocked down. Destroyed.

I struggle to understand what Jeremy is doing here,

or what has him so interested in the house in the first place. If he wanted the land, I don't see what the house has to do with anything.

With little else to do since Jeremy still has my phone, I lean against the porch and gaze into the forest.

It would be good to go for a run soon.

But the need to shift isn't overwhelming yet. And as alpha, I'm more in control of my shifts than a less dominant wolf.

The thing is, any run I go on will have to be with Jeremy since I doubt he's going to accept me going on my own. Not with his sharing a room and a bed mentality.

As I take in the lush greenery, I concede Jeremy wasn't entirely wrong about wanting to buy up the land.

Yet, how he's able to afford to buy it when he lives in t-shirts and jeans and has never mentioned working is beyond me.

He doesn't strike me as someone who's independently wealthy. Not that I'm about to ask him how he earns his money when he'll just mistake my question for interest. Which I'm not. Interested in him, that.

My wolf snorts, and I grind my teeth at the memory she shows me of my grabbing Jeremy and kissing him after my nightmare.

I had a reason for that, okay.

I shake my head as I tear my focus back from Jeremy and to the forest in front of me. It's mostly untouched and I guess that comes from the previous alpha Glynn Merrick being too lazy to do a thing about cutting back the trees or weeds.

It's wild, but kind of pretty too.

Talis' eyes would warm when she spoke about how free she felt running in the forest. As I take in the lush beauty in front of me, I see why.

There's something about it that calls to my wolf. Something about it that urges me to strip off my sweater, jeans, knee-high boots, and shift.

At a faint movement in the trees ahead, I freeze as fear wars with dread.

Slowly, I straighten from my lean.

There's someone there. A shifter.

I can feel eyes watching me, and I get the sense it's not just one.

It shouldn't come as a surprise to me that some of the Merrick pack might still be hanging about. Where else would they go after Dayne warned them to stay away from Hardin when they came looking for help from Talis?

Still, at nine in the morning, I wasn't expecting any of them to be in or near the house since they must have jobs in Dawley.

At the sound of more rustling, I start working out if I should go investigate or if I should go get Jeremy when a hand lands on my shoulder.

The sheer terror that grips me nearly sends me to

my knees, yet not a sound escapes my mouth. I've gone past the ability to scream.

"Hey, it's me," Jeremy says when I do nothing but stare at him.

I feel myself shaking and try to force myself to stop, only I can't.

Jeremy steps closer and wraps his arms around me, and that's what returns me to my senses.

I raise my hands between us and shove. Hard. "Don't…" I fight to speak, and my words emerge as a whisper as I glare at him, my heart still pounding hard enough to hurt. "Don't *ever* do that again."

He studies me for a long moment without saying a word, then he nods. "Okay." Then, as I'm working out what to say, he turns in the direction I was facing. "You saw something."

I fold my arms over my chest and nod. "I heard someone in the trees. Shifter."

As if the person was waiting for Jeremy to come out of the house, an older woman in worn clothing, dark hair with strands of gray, and a look of someone who's been trying and mostly failing to eke out a life for herself, emerges from the trees.

I recognize her scent as one of the shifters who came to Hardin looking for Talis. Maria, I think Talis said her name was.

"She isn't alone," I murmur, with my gaze fixed on the older woman hurrying across toward us with hope lighting her eyes.

Jeremy doesn't comment, and I turn to him. "Did you hear me?"

He ignores me in favor of stepping forward to the shifter with the hint of a smile on his face. "Hi, I'm Jeremy Stone."

"Yes," Maria says, darting a glance at me before she turns her entire attention to Jeremy as if I no longer exist. "You're an alpha. Are you going to start a new pack? I hope you do. Dawley needs a pack. *I* need a pack."

It isn't hard to tell from her lowered head, her inability to maintain eye contact with Jeremy, that Maria is a submissive shifter. Yet, something about her is...*wrong*.

She stares at the ground after she gives her little speech, and I narrow my eyes at her because I don't trust a single word that just came out of her mouth.

Jeremy turns to me, his face expressionless. "Savannah, perhaps you should wait in the truck."

I turn to him in disbelief.

He's ordering me to wait for him in the truck. As if I were a child. As if I'm in the way.

If that's the way he's going to play this, then fine.

"Give me my phone," I snap, holding my hand out.

Jeremy's expression doesn't change.

I say nothing else as I wait.

All I'm thinking is if he doesn't give me my phone right this second, I'm going to turn around and walk away, and leave everything behind. My clothes, my books, my purse, everything.

I will keep on running, and he will never find me again.

Not because the phone is that important to me. It isn't. It's what it represents. It's him using it to control me, and that is not going to happen. Not now. Not ever.

All the while, I feel Maria's silent attention.

Finally, Jeremy reaches into his pocket and withdraws my cell phone, which he places in my hand.

I close my hand around it, only he doesn't pull his hand away.

He bends his mouth to my ear. "The truck is unlocked. You had better be waiting for me when I'm done here."

Since there's no response I can make to that which isn't going to lead to an argument, I hold my tongue and wait for him to release his grip on my phone.

The second he does, I turn and walk away.

On my way back to the truck, I glance at my phone and see I have a missed call from my agent. Since I didn't hear my phone ringing, Jeremy must've put the call on silent when he was in the old Merrick house.

Alpha dick.

All I can say is I'm glad I didn't know about him silencing me phone when we were face to face because if I did, there'd have been a fight. And it would've been bloody.

CHAPTER NINE

*H*ours later, we're back at the rental, and I'm still stewing about Jeremy making me miss my call.

Even though I spoke with Paulo and learned the news wasn't good, the fact I missed it at all is something I can't let go.

But since Jeremy has been on the phone to the realtor about the Merrick property, and I was too angry to talk to him in the truck on the way back, I haven't had an opportunity to unload on him.

But I will. It's definitely coming.

Thinking it'll help me calm down, I head for the back porch because being inside with Jeremy is too much for me to handle right now.

Every time I see his face I want to kill him, and his scent is pissing me off because even after he took my phone, I *still* find it, and him, attractive.

I pace back and forth, grumbling under my breath all the while. Then I spin, about to pace the other direction, when I halt at the sight of something in the trees.

Eyes.

There, in the forest, someone is staring at me.

I stare back, unable to believe what I'm seeing.

Then I'm rushing back into the house, tearing my shirt off as I sprint up the stairs.

As if from a distance, I'm aware Jeremy is calling my name, but I can't absorb it, not when the only thing I'm thinking about is the need to shift, the need to hide.

I burst into my room and I'm struggling to tear my jeans off when Jeremy charges in seconds later and takes me down to the bed.

I fight him, I struggle, I scream, and all the while, he pins me down and refuses to let me up again.

After several seconds, or perhaps it's minutes of this, my struggles slow as I realize Jeremy isn't going anywhere, and with him pinning me to the bed, I can't shift.

Since any number of things could go wrong if I push myself to shift with him touching me, I fight the urge back.

I'm not about to risk being caught mid-shift or having my shift go wrong because his touch interfered with my ability to change all of me.

Finally, I lay still beneath him, out of breath, my

face pressed against the covers, and Jeremy stretched out on top of me.

I tilt my head to the side. "Can you get off me please, I can't breathe."

Without a word, Jeremy rolls off me before he shifts me to my back, and then he's on top of me again before I can breathe.

I stare up into his face and see his eyes have gone wolf.

"I'm not moving until you start talking," he snarls.

I open my mouth, completely unprepared for his anger.

"I don't care if it's big, or small, but you're telling me something. Right now."

With Jeremy laying on top of me, moving isn't an option since he's all muscle. So, I shift my gaze to just over his shoulder and try to sound casual. "I don't know what—"

His hand catches my chin and forces my gaze back to his. "Something has you waking screaming in the night, a nightmare so bad it took five *fucking* minutes before I could wake you."

Oh, that's bad.

He leans closer, close enough for me to see the rage burning in his eyes. "Now you're charging up the stairs, ready to shift and hide from whatever has you so terrified that all I smell is your terror, and once again, I can't reach you. *You. Will. Tell. Me. What. It. Is.*"

I flinch at each hard bitten-out word.

nothing funny about them. "Wasn't someone who should be an alpha," I echo quietly. "I suppose that's one way to put it."

When I turn around, I find Jeremy sitting with his back against the headboard, his entire focus on me. "Did he do something to you?"

I try to work out how to condense a lifetime's worth of pain into a few words, both mine and Talis'. "He hurt Talis. She was his niece. You met her in Hardin."

Something in Jeremy's expression shifts, and I get the impression he wasn't being entirely honest with me about what he knew about the Merrick pack.

I don't care enough to be pissed. If he wants to keep secrets from me, then fine, he can get whatever enjoyment from it while he can because it won't be for long.

"I'm guessing it wasn't an accident that caused her to be missing the tip of her finger," Jeremy says, his eyes sharpening.

The fact that Jeremy spotted that when Dayne was on his way to ripping his head off should surprise me, but it doesn't. I'm learning to accept Jeremy is far more observant than most.

"No. It was no accident," I murmur, thinking back to the moment a courier delivered a small package, followed by Dayne's destruction of the tree in the backyard.

I shake my head and continue. "This is the house we

stayed in when we came to rescue Talis after her uncle abducted her."

Jeremy gazes at me, and when I don't say anymore, he raises an eyebrow. "Why do I get a feeling you're leaving a lot unsaid?"

"Maybe because I am. Since none of it has anything to do with you, I think it's my right to decide what I'm going to tell you." I turn to leave.

"Take one more step, and you won't like what I do." The sudden coldness in Jeremy's voice lashes me to the spot.

"Don't threaten me," I snap, keeping my back to him.

"It's no threat, sweet."

I swing back to face him. "And stop calling me that. I'm not your sweet anything. I'm not your darling or your—"

"Mate?" Jeremy's voice is whisper-quiet, and something in his eyes has me taking a step back before I realize what I'm doing.

"No," I whisper.

The muscles in his arms tense as he propels himself off the bed in one smooth motion, and then he's stalking toward me with hard determination stamped across his face.

"What are you…" I back up because from what I see in his eyes, I know whatever is coming can't be good. "Jeremy…?"

I don't have a chance to finish my thought before

Jeremy grabs me and tosses me on the bed before following me down.

He grabs my shirt and rips the material off me, leaving me once again in my jeans and bra.

I gasp in surprise. "Jeremy, what are you—"

When he reaches for my jeans' button, I grab at his wrist.

Jeremy raises his gaze to my face. "Since you won't talk, I'm going to tear your clothes from your body, and then I'm going to bury my face between your legs."

I freeze at his words, and he lowers his face closer to mine. "I'm going to drive you to the edge of release over and over and over again until you're begging me. And you know what? I won't send you over. Not until you give me what I want."

Moisture floods my panties and Jeremy's nostrils flare as he picks up the scent of my arousal.

I open my mouth to deny it, to tell him it won't work, but we both know it'll be a lie because he's driven me to such highs that I was begging for him never to stop.

The thought he might take me there again and never let me finish is agony.

I won't hold out for long. Seconds maybe. Certainly not minutes.

My head falls back against the pillows and I close my eyes. "There was a man. A beta with eyes that…" I stop and swallow because I have no words.

Jeremy takes his hands away from the waistband of

my jeans and lowers himself over me, resting his weight on his elbows braced beside my head.

When his fingers smooth the hair back from my face, I open my eyes and glare at him. "This is a real alpha dick move, you know that, right?"

"I warned you I was ruthless about getting what I want. And right now, I want answers. Give them to me."

"I can't give you all of them. Not even if… not even if you do what you threaten. I'd rather die." I let him see the truth of it in my eyes.

If he pushes me to talk about everything, I'll find some way of getting free and I'd run and never stop running.

"I don't need all your secrets. Not yet, anyway. Tell me about this beta."

Not yet? How about not ever?

I wriggle as I try to get comfortable beneath Jeremy, but it isn't easy. "Are you always this hard?" I grumble.

His grin appears and disappears so quickly, it's a wonder I catch it at all. "Only around you, sweet. Now quit trying to buy time and talk."

After another heavy sigh, I fix my gaze on his chin since it's easier than looking into his eyes. Immediately, Jeremy's fingers bring my gaze right back to his.

"An assignment in New York got cut short, so I came back home early," I say, figuring that's a good a place as any to start.

Jeremy's gaze tells me to continue.

"I got a taxi back from the airport instead of calling anyone from the pack to come to get me."

"You don't drive?"

I shrug. "Sometimes. But since most of my work involves going to the airport and flying, it doesn't make sense for me to drive. When I need to go somewhere, there's usually always someone offering to drive me down to Hardin or take me to the airport."

He nods.

I swallow. "Well, I came back, and went straight to my cabin to shower and dump my stuff before letting everyone know I was back."

But that isn't the only reason. I always need time to work myself up to go to the main house. And the longer I can avoid it, the better.

As if suspecting I'm holding more back, Jeremy's eyebrow goes up, but I refuse to say anymore. What he's getting from me is already far more than I wanted to give him.

"I was getting the door open when I felt someone watching me. Even though I knew someone was there, I couldn't scent them. It was only later we learned he was using scent blockers."

I take another breath before I continue.

"And then I saw them. They were…" Words fail me for a second. "Torturer's eyes."

Even though I'm staring into Jeremy's eyes right now, that's not what I'm seeing. I'm back outside my cabin and I'm frozen with terror.

I grip onto the hem of his shirt because right now I need something to hold on to. I need something to keep me grounded in the here and now, when my memories are trying to drag me back into the past.

"It was like I could see all the things he wanted to do to me, and every single one of them was like a nightmare you couldn't imagine. They reminded me—"

Just in time, I stop myself.

Jeremy waits in silence for me to continue, but I blink the memory of Abel's eyes away and shake my head. "I ran to the house, and then I stayed there because I couldn't stay in my cabin anymore. Not after…" My voice trails off and Jeremy waits a few seconds, but when I don't say anymore, he speaks.

"But staying at the house isn't what you wanted to do?"

I wonder how he can read so much of what I try to hide from him, since no one has ever read me as easily as Jeremy does. "No. Staying in the house isn't what I wanted."

There's another silence as I try to figure out what to say.

"You saw something here," Jeremy prompts me, surprising me by not pushing at my reasons for not wanting to stay in the main house.

"I saw eyes watching me."

"The same eyes?" His face is expressionless.

I shake my head. "Not the same. He died. Dayne killed him. But he was there before. Staring at me through the trees." My eyes go to the window as I remember the eyes peering at me when I sat outside with Dayne. It didn't matter that I had Dayne beside me. The only thing that did was getting inside.

"Savannah." Jeremy's voice is mild, and I turn to meet his eyes when I realize the scent of my fear surrounds us.

"All I wanted to do was run away."

"Like now?"

This time, when I lower my gaze to his chin, Jeremy doesn't stop me. "Like now."

Jeremy presses his lips against my forehead, and for several minutes we stay like that.

"I suppose you think I'm pathetic. An alpha afraid of ghosts," I whisper, not knowing where the words are coming from, only feeling the need to say them.

"Ghosts have a power over us that it's impossible to turn away from," Jeremy says, lifting his head to peer in my eyes, "because they're in our heads. In our hearts. There's no unseeing them there."

What ghosts do you carry with you Jeremy Stone?

He's right. There isn't. There's no closing your eyes and willing them away, not when they live inside you.

But I don't tell Jeremy that. I don't say anything at all.

His gaze dips to my mouth, and I tense in anticipation of his kiss as I study the lines of his face. I fight against the urge to touch my fingers to his full lower lip, across his stubborn chin, and his straight nose.

Everything about him is strong, confident. He could have anything he wants. I look at him and I know it, yet he's determined to have me, only I don't know why.

I have a sudden awareness of him lying over me, his erection pressing into my lower belly. I want to tell him to take his shirt off, or else peel the white material off him myself so I can run my hands over his defined pecs, his abs, dig my nails into his skin.

But I don't. I don't do any of that.

I lay pinned to the bed beneath Jeremy and wait to see what he'll do to me. Kiss me? Fuck me?

When he rolls off me and rises to his feet, I blink at him in surprise, pushing myself up on my hands as I watch him stroll over to the closet. "What are you doing?"

"Getting that suitcase big enough to store a body," he calls out.

I frown and swing my legs off the bed to sit on the edge. "It isn't big enough to store dead bodies."

He emerges with it and dumps it on the middle of the floor. "It is."

When he crosses over to the bookcase, I watch him in silence before clearing my throat. "What are you doing?"

Jeremy grabs a handful of books. "Packing."

"Why?"

"We're staying somewhere else."

"But, why?"

Jeremy stops halfway through tossing my books in

the suitcase and meets my gaze. "Because someone was watching you from the forest. Until we know who that someone was, I'd rather we stay somewhere not as exposed."

When he says it like that, it makes a lot of sense.

Then I remember Maria. "But what about Maria?"

He shrugs and turns away to resume packing. "What about her?"

Although there are a million things I could say in response to his offhand question, I don't, because yet again I'm getting the impression there're things he's keeping from me.

Like the thing with the Merrick pack, and the sense he knows more than he wants to admit to me.

A part of me wants to push for answers, but the other part knows better.

In two days I'm leaving, regardless of whether I have anywhere to go, because being with Jeremy any longer than that is just too dangerous. *He's* too dangerous.

Not only that, but he's too good at exposing parts of me I'd rather keep buried.

CHAPTER TEN

"When you said we were going somewhere less exposed, I didn't think you were talking about the most expensive hotel in town," I say.

I feel Jeremy's eyes track me, the way they have since we arrived at the hotel several minutes before.

I wander around the large room, avoiding glancing at the king-size bed, which sits a few feet from a wall of glass, leading out to a balcony about half the size of the room itself.

Although I give the impression of being focused on exploring the room, I'm more concerned about keeping my distance from Jeremy whenever he ventures too close.

Since he pinned me down in the bed back at the rental, I haven't been able to stop thinking about him doing it again. But this time with both of us naked.

I should've known it was only a matter of time before those urges would wake up after all the hot sex we had in Chicago.

Back in Dawley, I was fine because I had my vibrator. But here? Even if I could've snuck it in my luggage without Talis or Regan seeing, it isn't like I would've been able to use it with me and Jeremy sharing a bed.

So, right now, the moment he approaches me, I find some reason to look at something on the opposite side of the room.

It's like a dance, and I know it's only a matter of time before Jeremy calls me out on my less than subtle attempts at creating distance between us.

"Is it? Well, it's got nothing on Chicago hotel room," Jeremy says from behind me.

I cross the plush, open-plan room in shades of gray and mustard and head for the balcony because it means I'm outside while Jeremy is inside.

I slide open the balcony door and step out onto a balcony lined with potted plants and a couple of striped loungers set in front of a small table.

Even though it's lunchtime and the streets below us are busy, we're up so high—the top floor—that the sound of traffic barely reaches us.

At the edge of the balcony, I rest my hands on the edge and gaze down.

It's beyond windy, and since I haven't bothered to tie my hair back, the wind whips it up and around me.

"You look like some sort of elemental witch."

I turn at the sound of Jeremy's voice and find him standing at the balcony doorway, studying me.

"Calling someone a witch isn't a nice thing to do," I tell him before returning my gaze to the world below me.

"It doesn't matter how far away you wander," Jeremy says casually.

I force myself to face him. "What doesn't?"

"I still feel it." His eyes never move from mine and something about the intensity of his gaze has my mouth going dry.

"Feel what?"

"Your need."

He can what?

I know how observant he is, and the last thing I want is for him to observe me.

I need to find some way to distract him.

"I don't know what you mean," I say, as I spin around and stare at the fast-moving traffic in central Dawley, trying to think of something to say or do to change the subject.

"It's been how long? Two, three months?"

I swallow hard as all thoughts empty from my head.

"Have you been touching yourself?"

Briefly, I close my eyes because I just…can't.

"Savannah?"

I shake my head because I can't look at him, and I can't speak. Both things will get me into trouble, I just know it.

"I know you must have. That or using a vibrator. Since I didn't see one in the luggage, and I know you haven't been touching yourself, I'm guessing you must be feeling pretty needy. Have you been hungry for my cock?"

I shake my head again, as my arousal simmers and builds.

How can he do this to me without even needing to touch?

When I hear him move, I tense, because I know what's coming.

He comes to a stop directly behind me. His warm hands rest lightly on my upper arms for a long moment, before he slowly slides them up and down my bare skin as I hold my breath.

When he stops, I let go of the breath. But then Jeremy steps into my body and lowers his head so his mouth is at my ear. "I've stroked myself thinking about you," he murmurs in my ear. "Tell me, have you touched your pussy thinking about me?"

I shiver, and my fingers tighten around the balcony railing. His scent surrounds me and I want to shift and roll around in it. I want to press my nose against his neck and inhale.

Why does he smell so good to me?

Jeremy moves his hands to my hips before he steps even closer, close enough for me to feel the hard press of him against me. I tremble.

"Tell me." His tongue touches the shell of my ear

and I whimper. "Do you think about me riding you hard as you touch yourself? Does it make you come?"

One hand leaves my hip and drifts around my waist, and I gasp when he jerks me hard against him.

I fight my body's response. But at the memory of him doing just that, the thought of him plunging inside me has me shifting restlessly against him.

"Tell me." He grinds his cock against my ass as he presses a kiss against my throat.

I whimper again, louder, unable to stop myself. "Yes."

I feel a smile forming against my skin. "Does it make you come hard?"

I shake my head. "No. Never as hard as…" My voice trails off.

His smile widens. "When I'm inside you?"

I don't say a word.

When he takes a step back, I try to squash down my surge of disappointment. Only Jeremy doesn't go anywhere. He grips my hips and turns me so my back is to the balcony.

For several seconds he studies me, then he lifts a hand and buries it in my hair blowing in the wind around us. "Maybe witch isn't right. Fae sounds better… all mysterious. Beautiful." His hand tightens, and he tugs gently, just enough for me to know what he wants.

I come to him because he's right, I am needy.

I lift my hands to touch his jaw and move closer, my

eyes fixed on his mouth. Jeremy lowers his head and I raise mine to brush my lips against his, just once.

My stomach clenches at that first touch, and then something in me eases. Our lips brush again, and I sigh as my eyes drift closed.

I want more.

"More," Jeremy groans against my lips, and my eyes fly open, startled at him saying exactly what I wanted.

His eyes are closed, and there's a peaceful expression on his face.

I shake my head, knowing he isn't reading my mind. No, this is just another thing I forgot about being with Jeremy in Chicago. This... connection.

We were so in tune that we woke needing each other. He knew what I needed—*exactly* what I needed—to send me hurtling into the most intense orgasms I've ever had in my life, and just a single touch would have me leaning into him for more.

And when I touched him, no matter where, his eyes would slam shut and he'd tense as if waiting for more, and I was always as hungry to touch him as he was for me to touch him.

I grip his shoulders as I close my eyes and lean in to kiss him again, still softer than what I want, but for now, it's what I need.

Slowly, he fists a hand in my hair as I deepen the kiss. I slide my hand down his chest and under his shirt, aching to touch his skin.

Jeremy lifts his head.

"Take it out," he murmurs against my lips, and tension coils at his words.

My eyes flutter open and find his gaze on my face, burning with need.

"Savannah…" His hands tighten in my hair and he tugs again, harder now, just on the edge of pain. My breath catches and his eyes darken in response.

"Yes," I murmur, as my eyes lock on his mouth, hungry for another kiss.

Jeremy tugs at my hair again, drawing my gaze back to his. "Take it out," he repeats. "I think it's long past time I rode you harder than this need's been riding you."

If I'd had any resistance left at that point, Jeremy's words would have well and truly burned them away.

I can see in his eyes that what he'll give me will be far and above anything my fingers or any vibrator ever will. With him, I'll have true release.

My hands go to his pants, and I tug his zipper down. I wrap my hand around his cock before carefully easing him out, as he groans low in his throat.

The sound goes straight to my core, and I tighten my grip around him, wanting to hear it again. With a harsh curse, Jeremy jerks my head to his and plunges his tongue into my mouth in a hungry kiss.

I stroke him, taking my time doing it as I re-learn his shape. All the while, wondering how having him in my hand can make me feel so good.

He deepens our kiss, burying both hands in my hair

and holding me still as his tongue teases each corner of my mouth. He kisses me with the same confidence, the same assurance that he knows exactly how to please me, and he does. He always has.

For several minutes we kiss, the wind whipping my hair around us and each stroke of my hand making Jeremy thrust against me with increasing desperation.

Without warning, he rips his hands from my hair and grabs for the hem of the sundress I changed into before we left the rental.

The second his hand closes around my panties, I tense because I know what he intends to do. Material tears and I gasp in his mouth, then Jeremy is tugging my hand away from his cock and lifting me into his arms.

I circle my legs around his hips and wrap my arms around his shoulders, moaning when the tip of his cock presses against my sex. Yet he doesn't move to thrust inside me. Not yet.

Our kiss goes on and on, feeding a part of me I never knew was starving until this very moment.

This is what I needed. Jeremy, just like this.

I grind myself against him, swallowing Jeremy's growl as his hands smooth up and down my back, over my hips, my hair, everywhere, as if he can't get enough.

I know the feeling.

I moan again as I lose myself in his kiss.

My back hits something soft. I startle and wrench my eyes open, surprised to find he's walked us inside.

I'm on the bed and Jeremy is easing his body down on top of mine, shoving at his pants as he does.

When I catch sight of what's in his eyes, my stomach clenches, and I start panting as the scent of my arousal intensifies. It's a look that makes me want to come.

His next kiss sends us falling back against the soft sheets as he pulls my dress up over my breasts and I push at his shirt so I can get to more of his skin. I need him skin to skin.

Jeremy's hands grab at my thighs, holding me open, and I wait with every muscle in my body tensed, desperate, for him to drive into me.

And then his phone starts ringing.

Jeremy freezes a breath away from slamming his cock into me. He breaks the kiss and from up close, our eyes lock. Neither of us says a word.

In that second, I realize what we're doing and that this way lies madness.

If we have sex, it's going to strengthen our mate bond. It'll bring us closer together when I should be doing everything to drive us apart, because if I don't, then it'll make leaving impossible.

"Savannah?" Jeremy's words are harsh with strain as his eyes search mine. And even though our bodies are still touching, it's like he can already feel me pulling away.

As I said, Jeremy is far more observant than I want him to be.

I pull my hands away from him and tug my dress down. "You should probably get that," I say, staring up at the ceiling since I can't bring myself to meet his eyes.

Jeremy leans over me and his cock glides along the seam of my sex, making me suck in a breath and my eyes shoot back to his face.

There's a fierce determination there, a ruthlessness he doesn't often reveal. It sits just below the surface of the smile he likes to wear.

But we both know the truth. The laughter in his eyes only gives the impression of him being easy-going. It fools the unwary.

I am no longer unwary.

I've made that mistake before.

"Don't move," he growls, a warning in his eyes. "I'll be right back." He presses a hard kiss to my lips before lifting his head.

The moment he rolls over and goes for his phone, I shove my dress the rest of the way down and move to slide off the bed.

A hand clamps around my ankle, and I freeze, my eyes going to his face to find him glaring at me just before he answers the phone.

At the sound of Maria sobbing, I yank at my leg. Hard.

If Jeremy thinks I'm going to lie here with my dress up to my neck waiting for him to soothe a fake-crying shifter that I tried to warn him was trouble, he's got another thing coming.

But I guess that was the reason he told me to wait in the truck at the Merrick house. All so he could play alpha to a shifter who stood by and watched as Glynn Merrick tortured Talis.

Jeremy glances at me with an unreadable expression, and I growl as I yank even harder.

This time he lets go, and I get to my feet before stalking toward the bathroom.

I don't stop to appreciate the beauty of the modern glass and steel space. I head straight for the large glass shower enclosure in the center of the room, pulling my dress over my head as I go, before stepping in and cranking up the dial all the way.

Under the spray that feels like fingers gliding all over my skin, I soon lose the battle against my arousal.

Shooting a glance at the steaming glass, I figure Jeremy will be on the phone for a while—probably a long while—going by Maria's wailing, and what I plan won't take long.

He won't know.

I reach my fingers between my parted legs, holding my breath just before I run my fingers along my folds, lightly rubbing as I imagine it's Jeremy doing it.

I release my breath and stroke harder, circling my clit as the pressure builds. I've lost track of how many times I've brought myself to climax in the months since Chicago, but no matter how many times, as long as I think of Jeremy, it never takes long to push myself over the edge.

When I first got back to Dawley, it was every night, sometimes twice, and no matter how hard I came, it was an empty kind of release and it never satisfied me the way I wanted or needed it to.

I touch my clit gently at first, then rub harder, reaching my free hand to squeeze at my aching breast, teasing at my nipple, needing more this time to send me over the edge.

Just as I come with a low moan, Jeremy shoves the shower door open and I meet his furious glare.

His eyes go to the hand between my legs and then the other on my breast.

"What did I tell you?" he snarls as he stalks into the shower. Never mind the fact he has his jeans half-undone, and he's still wearing his t-shirt, it doesn't stop him from stepping in fully dressed. Within seconds his clothes are soaked.

I drop my hands and back up. "Uh," I say, still struggling to come down from my release.

He corners me, and his eyes are dark with fury. "What did I say?"

"I… I—"

He steps closer, pulls his cock out of his pants, and presses the tip against my entrance. My eyes slam shut as I fight back a moan.

"Does it feel good?" he asks as he lifts my right leg at an angle.

"Savannah?" He grinds his cock against me and the blunt head of him edges inside me.

"Yes," I moan.

"You want the rest of my cock?" He presses a kiss to my mate bite that has me digging my nails into his hips and trying to haul him closer.

"Yes," I pant, "yes, I want it."

He leans closer, his lips against my ear. "Then next time, do what I tell you."

And just like that, he forces his body away from mine, and turns to walk away, leaving me shaking, and fully aroused all over again.

CHAPTER ELEVEN

"You're not eating," Jeremy says.

I tear my mind away from the shower incident the day before, and the hell that was sleeping naked beside him later that night.

I was so conscious of Jeremy lying naked inches away that sleep was pretty much impossible. My body wanted his, and no matter how many times I tried to convince myself otherwise, that wasn't enough to silence the ache inside me.

An ache that Jeremy has awakened.

I pick at the fish and salad on my plate in the hotel's restaurant and struggle to understand why I even bother to choose it.

I've never been the biggest fan of fish. Most wolf shifters aren't. We've always been more of the meat and potatoes kind.

Jeremy ordered two servings of the largest steak on

the menu and five different sides, which has pretty much taken over all the space on the table. But as this is a fancy restaurant with crystal chandeliers and a real pianist playing in the corner, the waiter didn't even blink.

"I'm not hungry," I tell my fish.

I know why I chose it. It was the first thing I saw on the menu, so I just went with it.

"You want to order something else."

Trust him to know.

"No."

"Are you *sure* you don't want something else?"

I lift my head at Jeremy's insistence, and when my eyes lock with his, I know he isn't talking about anything on the menu.

Is he being fucking serious?

I narrow my eyes. "No. There's nothing else I want."

Amusement lights his eyes as he reaches for his glass of red wine. I will him to spill it down the front of his white shirt. But of course, he doesn't.

"You sure about that, sweet? All you have to do is say the word."

Anger stirs, and I lean toward him. My whisper is low and furious. "Are you fucking kidding me? I am not about to beg you for your—"

Our waiter materializes beside our table with a warm smile. "And how is everything with your meal this evening? Is there anything I can get for you?"

I turn to him with a false smile. "I appreciate you stopping to ask, but I think we're okay. Thank you."

As I'm turning back to Jeremy, the waiter clears his throat.

"Are you sure, Miss Shaw? I can see you've eaten so little of the fish. The chef will be happy to prepare something else for you instead...?"

It takes a second for me to realize what's going on.

Someone has recognized me, otherwise why else would they be calling me Miss Shaw when I was only Madam before?

And now, someone has seen I'm not eating, and they're probably worried I'm going to slate the restaurant on Instagram or something.

"This is fine. Thank you," I say, with another empty smile, trying to ignore Jeremy's grin.

Of course, he'd think this was fucking hilarious. And the fact he has me swearing like this, even to myself, means if I don't get myself out of this situation, I'm going to explode.

"You know what, can you point the way to the bathroom?"

The waiter's expression turns to one of horror as he darts a glance at my mostly full plate before his eyes go to my stomach. "Oh, no. Let me—"

I yank the napkin from my lap and rise without waiting for him to pull my chair out. "I'm going to the bathroom," I tell Jeremy through gritted teeth.

"Don't take too long now, sweet." There's a warning

in his eyes as if he suspects I'll try to run, which makes me glare at him even harder.

Why is it every time I have the slightest thought about leaving, he knows it?

I reach for my purse. "I won't. If you'll just—" Instead, I watch as it disappears to Jeremy's side of the table. Just like the last time.

"I'm sure you won't be needing your phone for a quick trip to the bathroom, will you?"

As I consider arguing with him, I suddenly remember the waiter observing us.

So, I force another smile on my face. "Of course not, I'll be right back."

Without waiting for Jeremy to say anything else that'll only piss me off, I turn and stalk away, hoping I'm heading in the right direction since the waiter never told me where the bathroom was.

Five minutes in the toilet cubicle working on my breathing leaves me feeling like I'm not ready to kill Jeremy, and as I make my way through the foyer of the hotel and back to the restaurant, a man in a smart suit bumps into me hard enough for me to stumble and nearly go down.

"Hey, what—" I gasp and grab at my stomach.

When I look down, it takes me a second to understand what I'm seeing.

A circle of blood is forming on my pale green dress, dark and red. And as if my lack of understanding was holding the pain back, once I know what's happened, pain blooms.

I lift my head and stare into the man's face. "You stabbed me," I whisper.

He smiles, and steps closer, which is when I know he's going to do it again. His blandly handsome face gives nothing of his intention away, but a dark flash in his eyes warns me that this time he won't be going for my stomach.

This time, when his hand lashes out, I catch his wrist before he can plunge the small sharp knife into my heart, and as I stumble back in my heels, he follows to press me against the wall.

Since no one in the foyer reacts in any way, I guess it must look like we've bumped into each other and are moving to the side of the hallway to talk.

No one knows I'm in a fight for my life.

All because he's holding the knife low and stabbing upwards. Which means he must've done something like this before. Maybe even killed someone like this.

He's strong. A shifter. And he doesn't smell of anything, which means he's wearing scent blockers, a clear sign he must be a Merrick.

I open my mouth to scream, thinking the attention will draw him away, but then my vision changes. I snarl as my wolf attempts to force a shift, and I realize that drawing attention to us—to me—is the last thing I need.

If I shift in a crowded hotel foyer, there's no

knowing how bad things could get, so I push her back and stop the change.

"Savannah!"

Jeremy's voice pulls my attention from the shifter. I see him standing at the entrance to the restaurant with a frown on his face, as if he's trying to work out what's going on.

The shifter takes advantage of my distraction and plunges the dagger into me again, making me gasp in agony.

Although he missed my heart, wherever he stabbed me hurt like hell that it wouldn't surprise me to learn he hit an organ.

He yanks the blade out and prepares to stab again.

But before he does, I get a passing glimpse of a big guy with shaggy hair who barrels into the shifter hard enough that they both disappear into the crowd.

I'm too busy sliding down the wall to see any more than that.

That's when a woman starts screaming. She stares down at me in horror, and it takes one glance at the blood covering my chest for me to understand why.

I blink, and then Jeremy is there, his hands cradling the sides of my face as he gazes into my eyes with a fury unlike anything I've ever seen before.

"Jeremy," I whisper, "he stabbed me."

"It's okay, sweet." He scoops me in his arms before elbowing his way through a crowd that's coming to a standstill as they stare after us.

"Jeremy," I whisper again, clutching onto his shirt as the pain in my chest builds until it threatens to take me under.

My head is suddenly so heavy it falls back against his shoulder.

"Savannah!" Jeremy's voice is sharp. Full of command.

I open eyes I didn't realize I'd closed.

We're in a stairwell, and he's moving fast. Every step he takes hurts so much that I know I can't take anymore. My eyes flutter closed again.

"Savannah, stay with me. Open your eyes."

Only, no matter how much I try, I can't.

I hear him talking, and his voice grows more and more distant as if I'm falling down a tunnel and leaving him far above me. I never hit the bottom.

I just keep falling and falling until suddenly… there's nothing. No pain, no sound, no Jeremy. Nothing at all.

CHAPTER TWELVE

Pain rips me from the black nothing.

It's impossible to know how much time passes because all I'm conscious of is pain.

But at least I'm not alone.

As I drift in and out of an ocean of pain, Jeremy is always there, holding my hand, curving his body around mine, telling me to hold on, that it won't hurt for much longer.

And even though I know painkillers and drugs don't work on us shifters, it doesn't stop me from begging for them anyway.

Whatever Jeremy says is swept away before I can grab onto it like a lifeline, but it doesn't matter. All that matters is he's holding me, pressing his lips against my brow, and there's a burning intensity in his eyes that tells me he'd kill the world if it would stop me from hurting.

I sink back into blackness. Away from the pain, which I'm relieved about, and away from Jeremy, which I'm strangely reluctant to.

When I blink my eyes open, the sunlight streaming in through the open balcony windows tells me it's a new day.

The air smells fresh and clean, and when I glance down at my body, I'm covered in a thin white sheet. I don't feel I'm wearing anything else, not even my panties.

For once, my hair isn't trying to strangle me, or get in my eyes, or making me sweat because there's so much of it. When I touch my hair, I find it neatly braided, which makes me frown in confusion since I know I didn't do it.

Did Jeremy have someone else up here? Because I'm struggling to picture him braiding my hair. At all.

And someone must have undressed me and cleaned the blood from my body before slipping me into cool, fresh sheets.

Not someone, I tell myself, as I take in the figure slumped in a chair beside my bed.

Jeremy Stone. AKA alpha dick.

Except, he's not. At least not now.

I wonder how long that'll last.

I stare into his face. Well, as much of it as I can see, given he's sleeping with his jean-clad legs wide apart, arms crossed, and his head dipping forward so his chin is pressing against his chest.

Then I turn away and try to sit up.

Although most of my pain has subsided, there's still a sharpness where the shifter stabbed me the second time. When I lower the sheets and reach a finger to touch the still healing wound, I wince.

"I think he hit your kidney."

At Jeremy's voice, still husky from sleep, I lift my head from the wound under my left rib and turn to meet Jeremy's gaze.

His expression is blank. Like, completely neutral, no hint of a smile, or a snarl or... anything.

It's smooth as stone, and that's when I know how close I came to dying.

"Jeremy?" I whisper.

He lowers his gaze to the wound. "You were in so much pain and there was nothing I could do. No drug I could give you. No way to stop it."

When he falls silent, I take in his face and know he didn't sleep. "I heard you talking. I don't remember what you said, but I knew you were there and what you were saying made me feel... better."

Jeremy's lips twitch. "I was telling you all the things I'd do to the shifter when I got my hands on him."

An urge to yawn sneaks up on me and I fight it back, even as I lay back down, this time on my side so I can still see Jeremy. "I guess that's why then."

His eyes are warm when they scan my face. "Sleep. You're still healing."

I wriggle as I struggle to get comfortable. "A woman

was screaming," I remember, thinking back to the hotel foyer. "I'm surprised no one came up here to find out what happened to me."

Jeremy rises from his chair and climbs into bed beside me. He gently shifts me until my head is resting on his t-shirt covered chest. I close my eyes and let out a small sigh when he smooths a hand down my braid.

"People did. The hotel staff mostly. I said it was a private matter, that the woman had overreacted, and you'd be fine."

"And did that work?" I feel myself drifting back to sleep.

"Not really. When I threatened to throw them down the stairs, that seemed to work better. I'm surprised they haven't called the police, though."

I smile because that is so what I expected Jeremy to do. "If they do, wake me and I'll talk to them," I mumble, already more asleep than awake.

Jeremy snorts. "I'm not waking you for any reason. You need to sleep to heal. Fuck them."

"Jeremy?"

"Sleep."

"But Jeremy, who was the shifter with the shaggy hair," I ask, fighting sleep, as I remember the guy who likely saved me from being stabbed again.

His chest rumbles with his muffled laughter. "Shaggy hair?"

"Mmm. He saved my life, I think."

Jeremy stops laughing. "We'll talk about it later."

"Are you just saying that to shut me up?"

"Yes, sweet. Now go to sleep."

I open my mouth to argue, but the only thing to emerge is a yawn so wide, it makes my eyes water, and has Jeremy chuckling.

Sleep comes easily, and it's easy to sink into when I have Jeremy stroking one hand down my braid, and his other arm wrapped snug around my waist.

It's much later that day, around early evening, that the alpha dick makes his reappearance.

"I am not going to the toilet with you standing over me, Jeremy. You can wait for me outside."

Since I've slept most of the day, when I finally woke, it was because of a hollowness in my stomach.

Jeremy helped me slip into one of his t-shirts since he refused to grab any of my clothes after he told me there was no point in my dressing. After that argument, we just keep finding reason after reason to argue.

Jeremy glares at me mutinously and doesn't make a move to leave the bathroom. "What if you fall?"

I glare back. "Then I'll get up."

When he opens his mouth, I grip his shirt and tug him closer, then I rise on my tiptoes and press a soft kiss to his lips. "I know you're worried, but I'm fine."

His eyes are warmer as he smooths hair from my

There's no humor lurking in the depth of his eyes. Not now.

No. All I'm seeing is all alpha. And nothing I say, nothing I do, is going to make him back down.

His name fits, I realize. Stone. Hard. Unmovable.

I close my eyes and force a breath out before reopening them. "Can you let me up, I'd like to get dressed first."

For several seconds, Jeremy stares deep into my eyes. What he's searching for, I couldn't say. Only he must find it because he releases his grip on my chin and rolls off me.

I move to the edge of the bed and stand to tug my jeans back up. After scanning the floor, I realize I must've left my shirt on the stairs so I head to the closet to grab another since I'd rather be fully dressed before this talk.

Once I've pulled it over my head, I stand in the middle of the room with my arms folded, gazing at the window, too afraid to venture any closer in case the eyes are still there.

"Savannah, come here."

I shake my head. "What do you know about the Merrick pack?"

My question surprises him. I can tell because of the brief pause that follows my words. "Not much. There were rumors the alpha wasn't someone who should be an alpha."

I smile at his choice of words, though there's

face. "Shout when you're done, and I'll come and get you."

And after he brushes his lips against mine, he leaves.

For several seconds I just stand there, staring after him, amazed I got him to listen.

"It won't always work," Jeremy calls from just outside.

I glare through the door. How does he always know what—

"Because I know you, Savannah. And if you took a moment to think about it, you'd realize you know me too."

Since I have no idea how to even begin to respond to that, I don't bother.

Instead, I focus what little energy I have on using the bathroom, washing my hands, face, and brushing my teeth.

I hesitate over getting in the shower, but the thought of standing any longer doesn't feel like it's going to end well, so I slowly make my way to the bathroom door, favoring my right side more and more with every step. But before I can open it, Jeremy does.

He takes one look into my face and swears. "You should've shouted," he growls as he scoops me into his arms.

I don't respond because the stabbing pain under my rib hurts too much. So, I close my eyes and press my face against his neck as I try to breathe through the pain.

"That bad, huh?" he asks, sounding a lot less growly than he did a second ago.

I nod.

Once he gets me back into bed, he sits on the edge and stares into my face. "I could get some tranquilizer darts," he offers.

Once the pain subsides a little, I narrow my eyes. "You are *not* shooting me with a tranq dart, Jeremy Stone. I saw how sick it made Talis and you are not doing that to me. And anyway, it's hit and miss whether it would do anything, anyway."

Jeremy sighs. "I should've done it when you were out of it."

It's a struggle to get comfortable since it hurts to lie on my back, on my side, and the thought of lying on my front sounds like the worst position of all.

"If you had," I grumble, "I'd have made sure your face was the first place I aimed my sick."

"Classy, Savannah. Real classy. You want to get in my lap?"

I stop wriggling around and turn to him. "What?"

"You can't get comfortable, and I can see you don't want to sleep. I'm asking if you want to get in my lap."

I stare at him. "I'm surprised you didn't just pick me up and plop me on there like some kind of—"

"I wouldn't finish that sentence if I were you."

Although my lips twitch, I nod and slip my arm around his shoulder as he lifts me out of bed. To my surprise, he walks us over to the couch in front of the

TV and settles me on his lap before grabbing for the remote.

"What?" he asks. "You said I shouldn't expect you to entertain me."

Since anything I say to that will probably lead to an argument, I stay silent. Instead, I rest my head against his shoulder as he flicks through channel after channel.

"You hungry?" he murmurs as he strokes my hair with one hand before he settles on a wildlife documentary.

I shake my head. "I know I should eat, but not yet. It hurts too much to think about eating."

He presses his lips against my forehead. "I'll order something up in an hour if you want? Steak and potatoes. I'll even cut it for you."

I smile with my eyes closed. "I'm injured, not a child."

Jeremy kisses my brow. "Same difference. Shhh. You're making me miss seeing how animals hunt in the wild," he whispers loudly.

"Shush me again and I'll show you. Firsthand."

His body shakes with silent laughter as he strokes a hand up and down my back in a way that has me wishing he would never stop.

CHAPTER THIRTEEN

This time it isn't pain that draws me from sleep, but pleasure.

The firm stroke of a tongue lapping between my legs has me moaning as I hover over the edge of release.

As if sensing how close I am to waking, hands pin me to the bed and a tongue laps hungrily at me, as if determined to drive me to release before I've opened my eyes.

My thighs shake as pressure continues to build. With my climax seconds away, I burrow my hands into soft hair and hold on tight.

When the tongue edges up, sliding through my folds, and flicks over my clit, I gasp and my eyes fly open. I gaze down my naked body, beyond turned on at the sight of Jeremy, naked, with his face buried between my legs, his large hands holding my thighs open.

As if he feels my attention, he raises his head, and at the dark heat in his eyes, I swallow.

"How's your side?" His voice is that husky growl that pierces my core.

My side?

"What?" I ask when he bends his head and laps at me. My breath catches, and I fight the need to lift my hips and rub myself against him.

After another firm lick, Jeremy lifts his head. "Any pain?"

Oh, right. The whole being stabbed thing.

"Uh, I don't think so," I say, since the only thing I feel is pleasure between my legs.

His lips quirk. "You sure about that?"

I do a quick mental check. "No pain," I say, hoping he gets back to licking between my legs. Two licks would probably do it. Okay, one. I'm that close.

God, he could just growl my name and that'd do it.

"Good." His eyes light with anticipation.

"Jeremy, what are you doing?" My voice is little more than a thread of sound, husky with desire.

Why the hell am I still talking?

"Giving you what you need." Jeremy bends his head.

For no reason I can think of, I tug at his hair to stop him because… wait, there actually is a reason. I need to know this isn't just Jeremy trying to mess with me.

"And what do I need?" I breathe.

Jeremy kisses the sensitive skin on my inner thighs.

"What no one else can give you but me." He raises eyes filled with utter confidence. "Just me."

He nips me, and as I'm still gasping at the sting of his bite, he's already soothing it with a soft kiss. "Tell me I'm wrong, Savannah."

I shake my head because I can't. And when I don't speak, he lowers his head, his eyes still locked with mine, and then he draws my clit into his mouth and sucks gently.

My climax blows through me, and I throw my head back and scream, writhing as he pins me to the bed and continues to suck.

I'm still struggling to come down, still fighting for breath when Jeremy slides up my body and gazes down into my face, male satisfaction stirring in his eyes.

"No need to look so pleased with yourself," I snap.

He bends his head and kisses me, a soft lingering kiss that makes me sigh into his mouth. I tangle my hands in his hair and pull him closer as Jeremy settles more of his weight on me.

But as I'm curving one leg around his hips, he breaks our kiss and gazes down at me, a hand closing around my thigh to stop me.

"Be sure, Savannah," he says, his eyes serious.

I take my hands from his hair and put them on his chest, then I push.

Jeremy's expression doesn't change as he moves, and I follow, keeping my hands on him until I have him on his back and I'm sat astride him. Then I reach for my braid.

I keep my eyes on him as I slowly unbraid my waist-length hair.

Once, just once, his eyes go to my fingers in my hair. "What are you doing?" His voice is thick, and his hands grip my hips harder as he shifts his gaze to my breasts.

"Giving you what you need."

I can't say why I'm so utterly certain that he wants me with my hair loose around my face, but I do. I'd bet my life on it.

"You know, I wouldn't mind if you picked up the pace a little," he says in a voice harsh with strain.

I stop.

"In about two seconds I'm going to move, Savannah," he warns me as his hands grip my hips even tighter.

The thought of how much Jeremy's holding himself back has my fingers shaking as I go back to releasing my braid. Seconds after I've run my hands through my now wavy hair, he slams into me with a groan.

My eyes slide shut as I cry out at his thick length filling me.

For one second, he doesn't move as I hear him fight for breath. Then he slowly lifts my body off him, making me whimper as my muscles ripple around his cock.

My nails dig into his shoulders as he jerks me down

at the same moment he drives into me again, burying every last inch of him deep inside me.

"Stop," I cry out, struggling to breathe, every muscle tense. "Just… stop a second, okay. Stop."

"Fuck." Jeremy rolls us until he's braced over me. I feel his eyes searching my face as he smooths my hair back. "Savannah?"

I'm too overwhelmed to respond. It's too much, everything I'm feeling, having him inside me again. It's all too much.

Jeremy starts to pull out.

I wrench my eyes open and grab at him. "Don't move."

He stills, and the fear I see in his eyes bleeds away. "Fuck, Savannah, I thought I hurt you. What the fuck?"

I close my eyes and swallow. "I don't want to tell you."

"Well, you'd better fucking start." Despite his harsh growl, he presses a tender kiss to my lips and his voice softens. "Did I hurt you?"

As much as I don't want to, I sigh because I have to tell him. I can't let him think he hurt me when he didn't.

Opening my eyes, I shift a little beneath him and when he slips in deeper, my breath catches.

"Savannah?" he groans as I feel him growing even harder inside me. "Tell me because I'm going to move again, and I need to know I didn't hurt you."

I stare at his chin. "I forgot how big you were," I blurt.

He's silent. And then his fingers go to my chin, and he tilts my head up. I'm fully prepared for him to be all smug about me admitting he's big, but his eyes are serious.

"I hurt you."

"Not hurt. I don't mean physical…" At Jeremy's raised eyebrow, I blush. "I don't *only* mean physically, it's… I just forgot about…" My voice trails off, and for the longest time, he stares into my eyes.

"You forgot about what?"

I lift my hand and curve it around his jaw. "I forgot how good you feel. I forgot how you fill every single part of me. I forgot how overwhelming it was, being with you. I don't know how, but I did."

Jeremy's eyes flash with heat before he dips his head for a searing kiss that has me winding my legs around him.

As we kiss, he takes my hands one at a time, and lifts them over my head, pinning them to the bed, and then he lifts his head.

For several seconds, he stares down at me, an inscrutable expression on his face. "I dreamed of this, you know. You and me, just like this. You lying beneath me, all that beautiful golden hair spread out on my pillow and you staring up at me with that look in those incredible blue eyes."

I swallow. "What look?"

He lowers his head. "The look that says you're mine," he murmurs against my lips, and then he thrusts.

Moaning, I arch my back as my inner muscles fight to adjust to his size. He eases away before driving into me, my hips rising to meet his.

His body plunges into mine with increasing force as I tug at his hands, holding my wrists to the bed.

"Jeremy, let go," I gasp, fighting to break his hold.

At my words, Jeremy peels his eyes open, and I see they've gone wolf.

He slams into me again. "You're mine," he snarls. "Submit."

"Let go," I snarl back, even as I lift my hips to meet each of his thrusts. "I won't submit."

When he bends his head, his kiss is hard, angry. "You will."

He shifts his hold until he's pinning both my wrists with one large hand, and eases his upper body from mine, before sliding his hand over my breast and down my body.

At the first touch of his fingers against my clit, I suck in a breath.

Jeremy stares into my eyes. "Submit, Savannah."

I shake my head.

"Submit." His finger brushes against that bundle of nerves again, and I stop fighting his hold and eagerly lift my hips, telling him without words I want more.

"Submit." He rubs again, and everything in me stills.

Tension fills me and I'm shaking all over, as I stare up at him with wide eyes.

"Jeremy," I whisper.

As if that was what he was waiting for, he releases his hold on my wrists, grips my hips with both hands, and pulls back before slamming into me.

My climax explodes through me. I scream and writhe and fight against it, even as I grab at Jeremy and hold on as he hammers into me again and again until he growls deep in his throat.

At the harsh jerk of him spilling himself inside me, I cry out again as my body shudders with the force of his release.

I think I pass out or I fall asleep—I don't know.

But when I open my eyes later, the sky outside is hazy and darkness is setting in.

I'm lying on my stomach, the sheets at my feet and my hair covering me. I'm alone in bed, but Jeremy is close. I feel him. Smell him.

I stretch and rise before turning. And then I see him, sat in the same chair he was in before. This time he's naked, his eyes are on me, and he's sipping whiskey from a cut-glass tumbler.

"Jeremy, what are you doing?" I ask, sitting the rest of the way up.

His eyes dip to my bare breasts and he takes a long draw of his drink. "Watching you."

I arch a brow. "You realize how creepy that sounds, right?"

"If someone else were doing it, yeah. But it's me, and you're mine, so it's not."

"Right, whatever you say."

Jeremy doesn't respond. Instead, his gaze slides down my body and settles between my legs. "Touch yourself."

I feel myself flushing. *"Excuse me!"*

His eyes return to my face. "I want to know what you like, I want to see you do it."

I try to hide my embarrassment. "I thought you had a problem with it, after last time."

"I had a problem with you doing it when I had other plans. Now, I want to see. I want to know what you like."

"I thought you knew what I liked," I comment archly.

Jeremy says nothing else, just takes another draw from his glass before he places it on a side table beside him. He widens his legs and when I see where he's about to put his hand, I swallow.

"What are you doing?" I don't take my eyes from his hand, closing around his cock.

"Showing you what I like."

His grip is hard. Much harder than I held him before. As I watch him stroke himself from base to tip, I know nothing in the world could make me look away.

"Savannah?"

I imagine wrapping my hands around him; I remember how he felt in my hand. Hot. Hard. Silky.

I'm ready to demand a touch when I realize he's still talking.

"Hmm," I murmur, distractedly, chewing on my lower lip.

"Show me more."

More?

And that's when I realize where I have my hand.

For a second, I still, as in my lust-induced fantasy of touching Jeremy, I realize I did the very thing he wanted.

But since I've started, and he's started, I figure why the hell not.

I dart a peek into his face and find his eyes locked at the junction of my thighs.

With his chair nearer the head of the bed than the base, I hesitate for a second before I move.

I tell myself he's seen it all before. I mean, I woke up with his face buried between my thighs hours before, and that wasn't even the first time.

I stop when I'm laying the wrong way on the bed, the balcony behind me, and Jeremy sat in his chair in front of me.

After hesitating for another second, I widen my legs before planting my feet on the mattress with my knees bent so he can see everything.

His eyes don't move from my sex, and he grips himself harder. "Get a pillow for your head."

I blink at him in confusion until I realize what he said.

Once I've stacked a couple of pillows under my head, I return my hand between my open thighs and fix my gaze at his cock, already glistening with pre-come.

"Jeremy?"

"Hmm?"

"How many of these fantasies do you have?" I murmur as I rub my fingers through my folds.

"Too many for you to worry about me running out. Touch your breast with the other hand, the way you did in the shower."

I lift my hand to squeeze at my breast, teasing the nipple, which makes me sigh as I sink my head back against the pillow. As the pressure continues to build, my breathing turns ragged and I stroke myself harder, shifting restlessly on the bed.

With my release slowly creeping up on me, my attention turns inward as I edge my fingers closer to my clit, not ready to touch myself there yet, knowing the moment I do, it'll all be over.

"That feel good?" Jeremy murmurs.

I peel open my eyes and find Jeremy's gaze focused on my face as he strokes himself with increasingly jerky movements.

I nod.

"How good?" He asks, his voice gruff.

I rub myself harder as my legs fall open even wider. "I'm going to come soon."

My mouth goes dry as I watch Jeremy rise and stalk toward me, his hand wrapped tight around his cock.

"Not until I'm inside you," he growls, as he sinks between my legs.

As he strokes himself with one hand, his other covers my neglected breast, and he proves he was paying attention by teasing my nipple exactly as I did.

My eyes close as I sink against the pillow, and I feel the brush of Jeremy's hair on me as he lowers his head. He presses a kiss to my breast and growls. "God, I love the taste of you. And these pretty tits. Perky. Sweet. I dream of them."

When both of his hands skim over me, I know he's no longer stroking himself, and I sigh and stop touching myself because nothing feels as good as Jeremy's hands on me.

He turns his attention to my other breast, drawing a nipple in his mouth and sucking lightly as he massages each one.

As I'm moaning beneath him, I suddenly still when it hits me what he just said.

My eyes snap open, and I sit up. "Wait just a second. You call me sweet. I hope you're not saying it's because of my breasts?"

His grin is wide enough to be answer enough.

"Jeremy, you can't go around—" I stop speaking when he lowers his hands to my hips and holds me still before thrusting inside me.

"Oh my fucking *God*." I shudder beneath him, my head falling back, so close, so painfully close to exploding with just that one thrust.

I'm desperate for him to move, at the same time I'm desperate for him to never move again. To just stay like this, joined hip to hip, on the edge of the most incredible pleasure. Forever.

"Not God," Jeremy mutters, bending his lips to mine. A smile in his eyes. "Your mate. Jeremy." And then he drives into me again.

My release crashes over me as I scream and dig my nails into his shoulders.

I writhe against him, losing myself in a never-ending wave of ecstasy as Jeremy hammers into me with enough force that the headboard smashes against the wall.

All I can do is cling to him as he rides me hard enough that my back arches and another orgasm tears through me.

When he lowers his head and his tongue laps at my mate bite, I whimper my release as a strange daze settles over me.

He's killed me. Jeremy has killed me with sex.

I sink into the sheets as Jeremy growls deep in his throat as his cock jerks inside me, and with a soft sigh, my eyes flutter closed.

CHAPTER FOURTEEN

I wake early enough the next morning that most of the street below me is empty, and the sky is still a hazy gray as the sun crawls into the sky.

No matter how hard I try, I can't stop thinking about last night.

I slept with Jeremy, and I don't know what that means for me, for us, for everything.

I wasn't expecting him to still be sleeping, but I guess taking care of me took it out of him. So, for several seconds, I lay wrapped in his arms, fighting the urge to kiss him. A fight I would've lost if my stomach hadn't started rumbling.

After slipping into one of his t-shirts, I helped myself to a cookie and banana the hotel staff left in a welcome basket for us before venturing out to watch the sunrise.

With my arms crossed over the balcony edge, I rest my chin on my forearms and sigh as I think about how much of an idiot I've been.

I know it's only luck that sex didn't strengthen our mate bond enough for me to be reading any emotions from Jeremy, nor him with me.

I hope.

When arms slip around my front and I feel hot naked skin curve around my back, I'm not surprised.

"You sound like you're thinking too hard," Jeremy murmurs against my hair.

"Probably," I agree.

We fall into a not uncomfortable silence as the sun brightens the sky.

Then it's Jeremy's turn to sigh. "I thought I lost you."

At the soft note in his voice, I swallow as tears fill my eyes. "I'm just a girl you met in a bar. We're a dime a dozen. Easily replaceable," I say, working to keep my tone light.

"You don't believe that any more than I do."

No. No, I don't. This… whatever Jeremy and I have, is something else.

"Your feet must be getting cold," he says when I don't respond.

They kind of are since I've been out here for maybe thirty minutes, and in little more than Jeremy's shirt, it's not just my feet that are cold.

"Yeah," I whisper, my eyes fixed on the world

waking up all around us. "But I'm not ready to go inside. Not yet."

I feel him nod. "You want me to—"

Already I'm shaking my head as I grab onto his arm to stop him from going anywhere. "No. Just… stay for a while."

Jeremy's only response is a kiss on the top of my head.

"But if your package is in danger of falling off, don't be afraid of telling me. I'm kind of getting attached to the thing."

"Not as attached as I am, sweet," he murmurs, with a smile in his voice.

We stay out on the balcony for nearly an hour until I tell Jeremy I'm ready to go back inside.

He sweeps me into his arms and carries me right back to bed. And thankfully, his package didn't freeze and fall off, which I'm pleased to find out when he slips back inside me. I'd have been devastated if it had.

A soft thump hitting the pillow beside my head wakes me, and I blink bleary eyes at Jeremy standing over me in a pair of briefs. "What?"

"The hotel staff returned your phone since I, uh, might have left your purse in the restaurant when I came after you."

I grab it before rolling onto my back. Although I

could snap at him for it, I figure after everything he's done for me, it would be pretty pissy of me to bitch at him for forgetting my phone.

"Well, I hope you weren't aiming for my face," I grumble.

Jeremy's phone vibrates, and he wanders over to the dining table to get it. "Nope. Not this time. If I was, I'd have been standing further away from your claws."

"Nice," I say, surprised to see it has a full battery. "I thought it'd be dead."

"I charged it while you were sleeping."

"God, that sounds like a modern-day rom-com. Instead of Sandra Bullock, it's Jennifer Lawrence as a trendy young tech exec in Silicon Valley instead of… where was that movie set again?" I ask, not expecting Jeremy to know the answer since, well, he's a guy, and it's an older movie.

I scroll through messages from Regan, Talis, and Jenna. It's nothing interesting. Mostly it's them checking up on me and finding out if I still want to come down for a BBQ over the weekend. So, I shoot them a quick reply, telling them I don't know yet, but I'll get back to them.

"Chicago," Jeremy murmurs, sounding distracted as he taps out a message.

I stop what I'm doing to sit up and stare at him. "You're right."

As if he feels my eyes on him, he glances up from his phone. "What?"

"The movie was set in Chicago."

"Yes," he says slowly. "I know, I just told you."

"But *you're* not supposed to know that."

"Because I'm a guy?"

I flop back on the bed and go back to scanning through my messages. "Yes, because you're a—"

Paulo's text message silences me. *Start packing gorgeous. Guess who's going to Paris? XOXO PS. It's u with a capital U.*

He did it.

Paulo legit did it. He landed me the dream Paris job.

Why am I so surprised? And shouldn't I already be on my feet packing as I manically dance around screaming 'I'm free!'?

"Savannah?"

I stare at my phone. "Hmmm?"

"You okay?"

Jeremy. Shit.

I have to tell Jeremy I'm moving to Paris. Probably in as little as a week. I have to tell him hours after he saved my life, and held me on the balcony, and told me he thought he'd lost me with a catch in his voice.

"Savannah?"

At the sound of him coming closer, I drop my phone on the pillow before I sit up and start looking for my shirt. "Yep."

"You okay?"

I don't find my shirt, but I find one of his.

It's the same one I wore hours earlier on the

balcony. After a quick sniff convinces me it'll do, I tug it on. "I'm good."

By the time I'm on my feet, Jeremy is standing a few feet away, gazing into my face in a way that tells me he doesn't believe me.

Distraction might be in order.

I slip my arms around his waist and peer into his face. "Feed me," I whine.

Although I catch him glance back at the bed, he doesn't push me for details. "What do you feel like?"

I rest my head against his chest, since the less eye contact, the better. "Anything. Jeremy?"

He strokes his hand down the length of my hair. "Yes, sweet?"

"You're not likely to kill Dayne on sight, are you?"

There's a brief pause, as if he's weighing it up. "I don't know. I might. Why?"

Operation distraction is a go.

"Talis and some of the others in the pack want me—and I'm guessing you as well—to go back to Hardin for the weekend for a BBQ. I know alphas can't be around—"

"We'll go. And no. I won't kill Dayne if he does nothing to deserve it."

When I peel my head from his chest so I can glare at him, I find Jeremy grinning down at me. "What do you mean, if he doesn't deserve it?"

"As I said, sweet. Now. You ready for a shower before we get you fed?"

"I guess."

As Jeremy puts his phone down, I wonder at his message. "Was it important?" I ask as he leads us to the bathroom.

He shrugs. "Not sure yet."

His answer is so vague, it makes me itch to ask what he's talking about. But since I'm not ready to go poking around for answers to questions for fear that it'll lead to Jeremy asking some of his own, I keep my mouth shut.

I know it's only a matter of time before the Paris conversation happens. Until it does, I have time to figure out how to tell Jeremy I'm leaving him, and why it isn't filling me with the excitement I was expecting.

CHAPTER FIFTEEN

*T*he next day I'm no closer to figuring anything out, and I'm still not fighting to hold back my excitement at the thought of getting away to Paris and building a new life for myself. This is because there isn't any. Excitement, that is.

I lay with my back to Jeremy, staring at the wall, wide awake, but not ready to turn to face him yet or even to move.

When Jeremy wraps his arm around my waist and hauls me flush against him, I fight back my moan at how good it feels—how good it *always* feels—when he does it.

"Something's wrong," he murmurs against my hair.

For one second, I freeze because I guess he must know.

Maybe he took a sneaky peek at my phone while I was sleeping. I mean, he *did* say he charged it while I was sleeping. Which means there was nothing to stop him from scrolling through all my messages.

But he couldn't have, I tell myself since all the messages were still unread.

"You hear me, sweet?"

"I heard you." But I don't turn around. I don't move.

I still haven't replied to Paulo's message about Paris, and I'm going to need to do it soon because he needs to make preparations. *I* need to make preparations.

I could've replied after Jeremy and I had a shower together and he was busy ordering room service, but evidently, I thought napping followed by another round of sex was more important than securing my future.

And the sex.

The sex has got to stop.

Already I'm struggling to imagine what my life will be like without Jeremy in it, and I have no doubt it's because of our mate bond strengthening.

I have to stop having sex with Jeremy.

Yet even as I'm thinking it, his hand glides along my belly and angles down.

"Jeremy, what are you doing?" I gasp, grabbing at his hand a touch desperately.

"Getting you to talk," he murmurs.

"By putting my hand between my legs?" I lose the battle to stop Jeremy from touching me. Though if I'm being completely honest with myself, I don't think I was trying all that hard to begin with. It was a half-hearted attempt at best.

He kisses my neck, distracting me, and when he glides a finger against me, I jump.

"Screaming's a form of talking."

As I'm trying to process his words, he dips a finger inside me, making me moan. "Jeremy, stop."

He presses another kiss on my throat, softer now, as his finger continues to brush against me.

I moan again, a needier sound, and against my ass, I feel him getting harder.

My desperation grows, because I know if I don't put a stop to this right now, it's going to end one way.

"So you're saying you don't want me to touch you? You don't want me to slide my cock inside a pussy I know would welcome me in right this second?"

I hesitate.

Come on. I'm human, okay.

"Savannah?" Jeremy's voice is a low growl against my skin and has me ready to demand he fucks me. Yet somehow, I find the determination to shake my head.

What can I say? What can I say to get him to stop? Think. Think. Think.

"My side hurts," I blurt. Briefly, I shut my eyes after my big, fat lie.

His finger stops brushing against me, and he lifts his hand away.

I focus on wiping all expression off my face as Jeremy shifts me until I'm on my back. For several seconds, he does nothing but stare down into my face.

"Why didn't you say anything?" His voice is low, and the guilt I see stirring in his eyes has me forcing my gaze away.

"Savannah!" he snaps, making me jerk my eyes back to him. "Why didn't you tell me I was hurting you?"

When I see the anger in his eyes is directed at himself instead of me, my guilt multiplies by a factor of a hundred.

As if lying to his face wasn't bad enough, I make him think he hurt me? There's a special place in hell for people like me, I'm sure of it.

I start to tell him the truth. Only, before I can, Jeremy's phone rings.

Jeremy rolls over and grabs it from the side table before lying on his back to answer it with a snarl. "What now, Jackson?"

He's on the phone, Savannah. Now is the time to make your escape.

But of course, like an idiot, I turn to my side and watch him on the phone.

He's still angry, and his anger increases when the guy who sounds like he could be Jeremy's brother, tells him to hold off on our plan to go to the Merrick land.

We were going back? What for?

I have so many questions. Like, who's Jackson? Is he the shaggy-haired shifter who saved me at the hotel? Or is he a brother Jeremy's never mentioned before?

I frown as I consider that. Surely Jeremy would've told me he had a brother, especially if he was in Dawley. Wouldn't he?

Then there's the money. How is Jeremy able to afford this hotel and buying the Merrick land? What about his life in Chicago? Surely, he has furniture and more clothes there. Is he having all of his things shipped here?

When I met him in Chicago, he never gave off the impression of being wealthy, and he still doesn't. He's just like any normal guy. Normal apartment, normal clothing brands, nothing cheap but nothing expensive either.

But he drinks expensive whiskey, and he ordered one of the best wines on the menu after a brief scan of the wine menu at the restaurant.

Who is Jeremy Stone and why am I so fascinated by him?

As if Jeremy feels the weight of my attention, he turns his head to me as he continues his conversation, still flat on his back. Now that he's got his snarling out of his system, he seems content to listen to Jackson talk about the Merrick land.

He's so attractive to me. Everything I see, I like. Well, except for some facets of his personality, but his face, his body, the way he studies me with absolute focus, it calls to me.

The longer I examine him, the more Jeremy's

expression softens. When he reaches out and brushes a finger over my lips, I don't stop him.

I lean forward and press a soft kiss on his lips, and then his jaw, his throat.

He makes a soft sound in his throat that has me wanting him to make other sounds. So, like some kind of sex-starved creature, I completely ignore my plans to stop having sex with Jeremy and start kissing my way down his chest instead.

I feel his hand combing through my hair, and assuming this is a sign he wants me to keep going, I do.

His skin tastes so good. I kiss a lazy path down his defined muscles, feel them tense as I work myself lower until I'm lying with his cock in front of my face and the sheets are somewhere down the bottom of the bed.

I glance up.

Jeremy's grip on the phone is so tight, I take a second to wonder if it's going to survive much longer.

Our eyes connect, and without looking away, I close my hand around the base of his cock and bend my head to press a soft kiss at the very tip.

A fine tremble warns me of the tension racing through him. This time I'm not so gentle. I part my lips and take him in my mouth, alternating sucking and lapping at his tip.

His hips jerk as he thrusts reflexively against me, and closing my eyes, I use my hand to stroke up and down him as I try to take as much of him in my mouth as I can.

Even though Jeremy isn't touching me, I moan at how good it makes me feel to touch and taste him. He's like a drug and I want more of him.

I lose track of time as I take him deeper and deeper into my mouth. All the while, the hand in my hair, stroking, tugging, brushing the strands back from my face, becomes increasingly desperate.

I slide my hand down the base of Jeremy's cock to cup him in my hand. He makes a choking sound in response. Once he's released his tight grip on my hair, I hold my breath and swallow him so deep, the tip of him tickles the back of my throat.

From somewhere above, a crunching sound followed by a thump on the floor announces the death of Jeremy's phone. But before I can lift my head to see, Jeremy has both hands combing through my hair as he groans my name.

"Fuck, Savannah, you have to stop. I'm going to come."

I draw my head up, slowly releasing him, and lap at the salty liquid spilling from the tip.

"So, come," I murmur, as I prepare to swallow him again.

I have no memory of how he does it, but between one moment and the next, I'm under Jeremy and his hands are gripping my hips.

I blink up at him in surprise. "Uh, how did I—"

Jeremy lowers his head and gives me the most desperate, hungry kiss I've ever had in my life. It's so potent, I feel the impact of it right between my legs.

Who knew you could come from a kiss? Because a kiss like this? It'll do it.

He lifts his head.

For a second, I'm sure he's going to speak, but he doesn't, just gazes down at me. His hands tighten on my hips and with a gentleness I'm not used to from Jeremy, he buries himself inside me.

While I'm not against gentle, something about him makes me so hungry that more often than not, it's not enough. I always want more. I want hard. I want fast. I want it all, and now.

Instead of demanding more, I lift one leg and wrap it around his hips, so he sinks deeper into me.

"Jeremy," I moan.

He lowers his head and brushes a soft kiss against my lips. "Shhh, baby." He kisses me again, longer this time, as he strokes himself inside me. "Let me love you like this."

My eyelids flutter closed, and my head falls back as we find the perfect rhythm. Our pleasure, a slow building, simmering thing, builds and builds.

There's no urgency, no rush to get to the end. There's only the bliss of our bodies moving with perfect harmony with each other.

I moan at each joining of our bodies, and the sound

of Jeremy's low groans against my lips has me clinging to him all the harder.

Finally, I grab at Jeremy's shoulders as he tilts my hips the tiniest degree. The base of his cock rubs against my clit and I shatter with a sharp cry.

As I'm shuddering, Jeremy drives into me one last time. He groans and holds himself tight against me until I feel the hot spill of his release filling me.

With the same ease that he moved me before, Jeremy shifts us until we're lying side-by-side. I sigh and burrow into his warm body, our lips meeting in a lingering kiss that's more sweet than needy until my eyelids are heavy with the need to sleep.

I'm drifting off with my face pressed against Jeremy's throat when reality rears its ugly head. I just had sex with Jeremy. Again.

My eyes snap open.

Fuck, the mate bond.

CHAPTER SIXTEEN

"You ready to tell me about the nightmare that had you up most of the night?"

I wrap my arms around my raised legs and shake my head.

It's early. Not even five yet, and the thought of getting back into bed with Jeremy is not part of my future. I refuse to let it. Not again.

So, I'm in another one of his shirts while I sit in front of the TV, though I haven't bothered to turn it on. I thought it might wake Jeremy, but I should've known it wouldn't matter if I had the TV on or not. He always knows when I'm not sleeping beside him.

"It can't be that bad, can it?" Jeremy doesn't bother with the couch. He parks himself on the coffee table in front of me and lowers his head, so we're eye to eye.

He's been so nice to me in the two days since I gave him a blow job.

While I'd like to think it's because I was just that good, I know it's not that.

There's a softness in his eyes when he looks at me, and I know the reason Jeremy isn't out in Dawley hunting the shifter who stabbed me is that he doesn't want to leave me alone.

The day after he destroyed his cell phone, Jeremy had the concierge order him a new one and have it sent up to our room. That's how serious he is about staying with me, and it's making me realize I've let things go further than they should.

Everything is happening all at once.

Contracts for the Merrick land sale arrived for Jeremy to sign.

We're supposed to be going back to Hardin for the BBQ and everyone will be expecting to see a happily mated couple still in their honeymoon period.

I still haven't told Paulo I'm accepting the Paris job that I'm supposed to be getting on a flight late next week.

I'm getting more flashbacks, which means the worst of my nightmares about Owen aren't too far away.

And last night I had a dream I was pregnant.

My scent hasn't changed, so I know it hasn't happened yet, but experience has proven that the only contraceptive good enough to prevent a shifter pregnancy is to stop having sex.

I think back to Talis, who found out about her pregnancy at the worst possible time after she and Dayne had only been together for a couple of weeks. Which means it could happen just as suddenly to me.

"Savannah?"

I blink to refocus on Jeremy sitting on a glass coffee table in nothing but a pair of jeans, and his eyes creased with concern.

I swallow hard. "I'm leaving."

His face turns expressionless as he sits up. "To go?"

"Paris," I say. "For work."

"And this job? How long will you be gone?"

"Six months."

"But…"

Why is this so hard? And how does he always know when I'm holding something back?

"It's looking like it'll be longer."

Again, his expression doesn't change. "How much longer?"

"The forever kind of longer."

At this he blinks, then he nods as if this isn't news to him. "I'm guessing this is the plan you meant back in Hardin."

It takes me several seconds to understand what he means because Hardin seems like so long ago. A lifetime. When I do, I nod. "Yes. So, it's probably for the best that we put an end to things now."

Jeremy's eyebrow goes up. "Put an end to things?"

Okay, so maybe you could've phrased it a little better than that, Savannah.

But as it's the truth, I nod.

"I'm guessing this is the reason for you pulling away?"

I frown. "What do you—"

He leans closer. "You think I can't tell when someone's pulling away from me—when my *mate* is pulling away?"

"Look, I told you this wasn't what I wanted, and I still don't."

"I see."

"I mean, you're buying the Merrick land," I say, trying to sound positive. "And you have Jackson, whoever that is, and I'm sure before you know it, you'll be alpha of a pack in Dawley and any woman would be happy to mate with you."

"Any woman except you, that is?"

"Jeremy, please don't make this harder than it needs to be."

At my words, his expression darkens. "So, I'm supposed to just let my mate walk away from me, and do nothing, say nothing. Make it *easy*?"

My anger stirs. "You bit me, okay? You didn't ask me what I wanted or tell me you planned on doing it. You just did it. I'm sorry, but this is happening. I'm going to Paris."

"Then why didn't you tell me days ago, when you found out you got the job?"

I go still at his question. "What?"

"You got the news days ago when I gave you your

phone. But you lied and said something about the BBQ in Hardin."

"You read my messages," I snarl.

I knew it.

Jeremy leans closer. "I didn't need to. I read *you*."

"What?"

"I know you, Savannah. I know your expressions. I know when you're trying to hide something from me. I know when you're lying to me. I didn't need to read your messages to know what was going on. And you think you're leaving? It's too late for that. Far too late."

At his words, I fall silent, because he's right. Jeremy has always known when I'm hiding things from him. I don't know how, but he has.

After a pause, I clear my throat. "Well, it doesn't change anything. I'm still leaving."

I move to stand, figuring there's no time like the present to start packing.

"No."

For a second, I stare at him in amazement. "I'm sorry, but what?"

"I said no," Jeremy says casually. "You're not leaving me. I refuse to let you."

"Unfortunately," I bite out, "that's not up to you. You can't stop me."

His eyes lighten and I know it's his wolf staring back at me. "You wanna bet on that?"

"You can't stop me, Jeremy."

"Yes. I. Can."

We stare at each other, and I realize something then. I should've run when I had the chance because something in Jeremy's eyes warns me that he never will.

Over time, regardless of what I want, he'll twist me into the thing he wants. The mate he wants. We'll move into the Merrick house, and he'll be alpha, and I'll be Luna of a pack I never wanted.

Before too long, I'll be pregnant and then leaving will truly be impossible, and as the days go by, and then months, my nightmares will return, and I'll find myself more trapped with him than I ever felt in Hardin.

Except I won't have Dayne there. I won't have anyone who understands even a hint of what I went through, and I will rebel against telling Jeremy.

Eventually, Jeremy's patience will snap and he'll force me to tell him everything, and I will. And then what'll start as resentment will turn to hate.

It will kill me.

Or one night the nightmares will.

There's one way to stop it. Only one. My heart clenches in pain, but I ignore it and force myself to speak the words.

"Jeremy Stone, I reject—"

Jeremy claps his hand over my mouth and takes me down onto the couch.

I struggle to push him off, to peel his hand off my

mouth, but my strength, my anger, is nothing compared to the fury I see burning in his eyes.

"You fucking dare!" he snarls.

No matter how much I shove at him and push, nothing can move him. Somehow we end up on the floor, wrestling, fighting, snarling as I battle to get free as he keeps me pinned.

If Regan could see me now, she wouldn't recognize me. No one in Hardin would.

I've always fought to stay calm, to keep all my demons, all my rage buried so deep inside me that no one knows it's there.

This time I let it out.

I fight.

I get a hand free and lash out, opening up a cut on Jeremy's chest. He grabs my shirt and rips it from my body. I scream and try to twist free of his hold as my hair blinds me.

Jeremy hauls me up from the floor and presses me facedown on the couch while he's tucked behind me.

I kick back at him, but he shoves a muscled thigh against my leg, pins my wrists to the couch and leans over me. "You done?"

I fight to catch my breath but don't respond.

"Savannah," Jeremy snarls. "Have you got that out of your system?" He bites out.

I test the grip he has on me. And finding it absolute, I nod.

"Good. Now I'm going to undo my pants, tear your panties off you and slide inside you."

And just like that, I'm ready to come at his gruff words.

"I'm guessing you don't have a problem with that," he says, inhaling, his voice gone husky.

His grip around my wrists loosens a touch, and the second it does, I struggle.

Jeremy's hands tighten, so suddenly that I know he was just testing me.

"I fucking hate you," I snarl, tears filling my eyes. "I hate you," I whisper.

He kisses my throat. "Hate? No. You're not stupid, Savannah. Open your eyes."

"I do. I hate you."

"Stop me, then, Savannah. Stop me." And then he lets go, just lets go of my wrists and I start moving, as he leans away from me.

But then I hear his zip, and I stop. Anticipation races through me.

He's undoing his pants, just like he said, and then he's going to…

His hand closes around my panties, and I hold my breath as I wait.

Material tears and I gasp.

"Savannah, if you hated me, you'd be stopping me about now." Jeremy's weight returns, his body curving around mine as we kneel in front of the couch. His lips return to my throat, and his hands slide up my arms and to my hands. "So, stop me."

This time, his hands don't pin me. He links them with mine, and I grip him back as I rest my right cheek against the fabric couch.

"Stop me," he whispers against my skin, as I feel the press of his cock against my ass.

I shake my head, even as I'm leaning forward so the tip of him nudges me. "Jeremy, please."

"What?" He presses even more of him against me. "What do you want, Savannah?"

I close my eyes and push back against him. Jeremy edges away and I make a sound of frustration.

"Tell me. I need to hear you say it."

And I can tell that he does. I hear the strain in his voice, hear the harshness of his breath, as if he's barely holding himself together. I understand the feeling.

I'm so close to the edge. "You. I need you."

"You need your mate," he groans as his cock nudges me again.

I moan as he invades me one slow inch at a time, and once he's deep within me, he stops moving. We lie still, our breathing sounding overly loud in the quiet room.

"Are you ready for me, sweet?" Even as he's asking, Jeremy is easing his body away from mine, and I know what's coming.

I feel myself clenching tight around him because

this is what I need, him like this. Fierce. Hungry. Desperate.

"Not like last time," I moan, as I shift restlessly. "I need—"

Jeremy doesn't wait for me to finish my sentence. He surges so deep that he touches the end of me and even then, it's not enough.

I shove back hard to meet him. *"Yes*, please I need—"

He hammers into me again, hard enough to silence me. "You never need to tell me how you need me," he snarls, as his body pounds into mine. "I will always know what my mate needs."

And then I lose the ability to speak as he gives me everything I need and more.

We fill the room with the sounds of flesh hitting flesh, low moans, and harsh groans.

Even though Jeremy's slowly but undeniably driving me toward a climax that has me seriously concerned that someone is going to hear my scream, that isn't enough to stop me begging for more.

I widen my stance and he slips a little deeper inside me. Jeremy swears so loudly in my ear that I know he's close, as close to climax as I am.

He slips one hand from mine and reaches between my legs.

One touch.

All it takes is one touch of my clit and I shove my face against the couch and scream so loud it isn't enough to silence me as I explode. My body undulates under a wave of pleasure so intense that I lose all awareness of everything except Jeremy's body driving into mine.

"Mate," he snarls in my ear, and then his hips slap against mine one last time before he growls as he jerks inside me. "Forever."

CHAPTER SEVENTEEN

*J*eremy's fingers trail a path up and down my bare arm. "I have to go out."

It's hours later, around midday I think, and Jeremy and I are back in bed after sex on the couch, the room service he ordered up, followed by more sex in bed.

I'm back to staring at the wall, and he's curved behind me. A veritable wall of heat.

"If you have to," I murmur.

"No trying to run."

At his words, I turn. I'm not angry anymore. I'm not sure what I'm feeling.

For several seconds, I study Jeremy without saying a word. "Why are you so sure I don't hate you?"

He slides his hand around my nape and leans forward to press a kiss to my lips that I return instantly, with no hesitation.

When he pulls back, he's smiling. "Because I know how you feel about me."

He rises from the bed, and I watch him step into his jeans, trying to ignore my body's response to his nakedness.

"And how do I feel about you, Jeremy Stone?"

"How about we talk about it when I get back?"

"Talk about what?"

"Us. I'll bring Jackson over, so you can meet him."

At the shifter's name, I nod. I'm guessing, from the conversations I've overheard, that this shifter—this Jackson is going to be his beta and has been at the Merrick land. "Is he the shifter with the shaggy hair? The one from the hotel foyer?"

And likely the one who saved my life.

Jeremy's eyes darken as if he's remembering it too, only he shakes his head as if he doesn't want to. "Later. If we get into it now, I'll never leave, and I need to."

I lay back down again as I think about that.

The fact Jeremy is talking about the future like that, talking about my feelings with that smile on his face, means he's likely started reading my emotions through the mate bond, even if I still can't read him.

Only, I don't feel anything. All I have to hold on to is my fear about the future, a certainty that my nightmares are waiting for me around the corner, and the sense that I've missed my chance to run.

If I left, Jeremy would find me in hours.

I was a stranger in Chicago, and he tracked me down to small-town Hardin in a couple of months.

There's no doubt in my mind that he will find me.

I could try rejecting the mating again, but the thought fills me with a pain I'm not ready to embrace. Making myself do it before was hard enough that I don't think I can again.

"You're thinking too hard," Jeremy says, perching on the edge of the bed in a t-shirt, jeans, and boots.

He smooths the hair away from my face as I stare up at him. "How can you be so sure everything will work out? How do you know?"

"Because I have you."

I can't even begin to understand what he means.

"But we want different things. You want to be alpha of your own pack in Dawley, and I want…" My voice trails off.

"Do I?" Jeremy asks, wearing an unreadable expression. "You sure about that, sweet?"

"Well, yeah. Why else are we here?"

"Why indeed?" He bends and presses a kiss to my lips. "How about you think about that, and think about what *you* want while I'm out, 'cause this isn't the first time I'm sensing you're not as sold on this Paris thing as you'd like me to believe?"

I open my mouth to deny it.

"Just think about it. And we'll talk. I'll even park the alpha dick attitude outside while we do it."

My lips curve in a reluctant smile. But then I

remember what my life is going to look like, and how trapped I'll be in Dawley. And then there are the nightmares.

My smile falls away and I sigh.

Jeremy examines me in silence for a beat before speaking. "We're so good at the sex, I think we skipped over the rest of it, didn't we?"

I blink up at him. "What?"

"The talking and the listening part."

Since I never expected him to be the one to bring it up, I don't really know what to say, even if what he's saying is true.

We don't talk.

We have hot sex that makes me crave him more and more, and we might joke a little with each other, that's it. Mostly we fuck, or we argue. Which is… weird that I never picked up on that before.

I sigh again before turning over, pretending that I'm going back to sleep. "Well, that's what you get when you mate some random hook-up in a bar," I tell him. "An unhealthy relationship."

"Random hook-up, huh?" Jeremy murmurs, bending down to kiss my neck.

Then, before I can stop him, his hand lands on my ass hard enough to hurt.

"Hey! Don't do that again."

He rubs the sting of his slap away, even as I'm shoving at him. That and trying desperately to hide the tiniest spark of arousal at him doing it.

"Play your cards right, and I'll kiss it better."

I pause to consider just what he intends to kiss better, but then he presses another kiss on my brow this time and rises.

"Where are you going and why aren't I coming with you?" I shout belatedly before he steps out.

When Jeremy turns around, his eyes are glinting with an intensity that makes me nervous. "I have to see to something. Won't take long. Sleep. Order room service. I'll be back soon."

For five minutes, I lay in bed thinking about where Jeremy went, and whether it has anything to do with the guy who stabbed me since there was more than a hint of hungry anticipation in his eyes.

I decide to get up and grab a shower since it feels like all I've been doing lately is sleep. That or have sex with Jeremy.

As I'm in the shower, I think about all the things that happened in Hardin, and about how I failed Dayne, and how I failed the pack. Yet I'm now going to be put in the position of leading one as Luna?

Although Dayne never blamed me for what happened, I was the only alpha in the house, and I was the only one to survive. It shouldn't have been me. I should've fought to my last breath to save Bridget and Angel and the others, but I didn't.

I don't deserve to be in any pack, least of all to be responsible for one.

And to think that I snapped at Talis when I let the weakest of our pack die.

Not die. Killed. And you didn't do a thing to stop it.

I bow my head against the shower wall as the tears fall.

Finally, minutes later, once I've I feel all cried out, I finish up my shower and return to the bedroom to dress in jeans, a cotton blouse, and a pair of boots.

It doesn't take long.

I don't bother drying my hair. It'll take too long. So, I run a brush through it and quickly braid it.

Stopping to do my makeup feels like too much of a waste of time when Jeremy could be back any minute, so I ignore the few bits of makeup I brought with me from Hardin.

It takes even less time to grab my purse and stuff it with my phone, a couple of changes of clothes, and then I force myself to walk to the front door and step out.

I'll be doing Jeremy a favor.

I can't be the Luna he and his pack will need, so I'll leave. And he's right about this Paris job. I don't know if it's what I want, so I won't go. Even if it was, I couldn't now anyway, not when Paris will be the first place Jeremy will look for me.

If I hide well enough, then maybe he'll look for me for a couple of months, and then the needs of his pack will call him back and he'll return to Dawley, meet some nice shifter girl, and he can build a life for himself without me.

Yet why does the thought of Jeremy being with someone else feel like being stabbed all over again?

Although the staff manning the front desk look surprised to see me, no one tries to stop me as I step out and start for the line of taxis in the distance.

A car starts up beside me, and the door swings open. "Excuse me, I'm looking for a restroom," a woman says. "Can you help?"

I turn to her with a smile. "Sure, there's one—"

A woman with a short dark bob and mean eyes stabs me in the arm with something sharp. I suck in a breath and start backing away, only I don't get far. The world turns hazy, and I get a sick feeling in the pit of my stomach.

Then I realize the woman has no scent.

Merrick pack.

I sag, and she wraps her arm around me and shoves me in the car idling beside her.

I don't know if it's her or someone else who stabs me in the back of my neck as I fight to get up.

With a soft sigh, my eyelids flutter shut, and everything goes black.

CHAPTER EIGHTEEN

When I open my eyes, I wake to find myself in a place so devoid of light, it's as if my eyes were still closed.

There is no way for me to gauge what time it is, let alone what day.

All I know is that I feel like I'm going to throw up because my stomach is churning like crazy, which means the woman—the shifter—hit me with tranquilizer darts.

Slowly, I sit up, trying not to move too quickly for fear of throwing up over myself, which is when something small and furry rubs up against my leg and its tail lashes against me.

With a sharp indrawn scream, I yank my foot away and the thing, I'm trying desperately not to think it's a rat, scurries away. And as if it and all its other buddies were just waiting for me to wake up, I hear them scurrying around, making me shudder in disgust.

I'm in a basement, but it's nothing like the Blackshaw basement where Dayne holds the pack meetings. No, this is a true basement with exposed brickwork at my back, a moldy smell, and other smells that aren't as pleasant.

I pick up the scent of old sick, and terror, and it isn't hard for me to guess that at some point Glynn Merrick, the previous, and now dead alpha of the Merrick pack once kept Talis here.

Since Dayne tore him to pieces, I know it isn't him behind my stabbing and abduction. But his pack, or rather, the remnants of it, must have some kind of plan to get revenge on the nearest Blackshaw, which just happens to be me.

I go still at the sound of someone undoing a latch from up high, and seconds later, I'm nearly blinded when the door creaks open and light floods in.

Turning my head to the side, I raise my hand to shield my face, and through eyes narrowed to slits, I get my first glimpse at my prison.

It's as dire as it smelled, with nothing except moldy walls and rat droppings on the ground.

I don't even want to think about what I might be sitting in, so I don't look down too long.

"Awake? Good. I'm going to need you to do something for me."

I lower my hand as my eyes adjust to the bright

light streaming into the dark hole someone's left me in. At the top of the stairs is the same petite woman with a short dark bob standing alongside the older shifter I didn't trust. Maria.

"Yeah, you're wasting your time. I'm not helping you do a damn thing," I say, forcing myself to remain calm.

The woman's face twists into a nasty scowl and I take a moment to feel sorry again for Talis because even though it's been less than a minute, I've seen enough of this woman to know she's a bitch with a capital B.

"Well. We might have to send Chris down there and see if carving bits off you doesn't make you a little more friendly."

I firm my jaw and raise my head. "Well, it's up to you, of course," I say, guessing who Chris might be. "But it's hardly a tactic that turned out well for your former alpha, now did it?"

The woman's eyes shift, and she snarls viciously.

I don't respond. I just continue to gaze up at her calmly.

Maria inches closer to the woman. "Loren, please. This isn't going to work, we should just—"

The shifter with the bob—Loren, I'm guessing—swings around to Maria and snarls in her face. "What? Go back to scurrying around in the dirt? No. They put us in this position. They will damn well fix it."

Spotting an opportunity to turn them against each

other, I clear my throat and wait until I've got their attention. "You should listen to your friend, Loren. As soon as Jeremy finds me—his mate—gone, it won't take him long until he figures out where I am, and then…" I shake my head because there's no need for me to explain how an alpha will react in a situation like that.

I'm not prepared for Loren's chuckle. "Really? Yeah, I don't see that happening. Not with you being seen leaving the hotel with a bag. And Maria here has filled us in on the problems you two are having. He'll think you've run. Right up until we start sending him pieces of you. Bigger, I think, than the finger Abel cut off Talis. We need to make a point."

Shit.

She's right.

Jeremy will find me gone. He'll see my bag and phone missing, and when he asks the front desk about me, they'll tell him I left and was last seen heading for a taxi.

There is no way he'd believe the Merrick pack has kidnapped me.

At my silence, her smile grows. "As you can see, we have things all worked out. So, rest up, and once Chris returns, we'll take our time picking out which part of you to send to that alpha of yours."

She turns to leave, and I grow desperate at the thought of being left in here for hours. "Wait! What do you want? I mean? Money or a new home, what?"

Loren stops at the entrance of the door and looks over her shoulder at me.

"Money would be nice," she says slowly. "A place would be even nicer. But you know what would be better than that?"

"I don't know," I say, getting a bad feeling.

She grins again and steps out, shoving Maria hard enough to send her stumbling as she goes. "Revenge," she says, and slams the door shut, plunging me back into darkness.

CHAPTER NINETEEN

I'm standing with my back pressed against the wall beside Angel's room, and when I look down, I see a pool of blood forming under the door.

It's been weeks since I've had this nightmare, and my heart thuds painfully loud because it's one of the worst.

Even though I know what I'll find inside, even though I'm screaming in my head not to reach out and push the handle down, I do.

It's as if my body and my mind have disconnected. All I can do is watch as, in slow motion, my hand reaches for the handle and closes around the metal, and just like always, it's cold.

I swallow hard, just as I always do, right before I squeeze.

Someone calls my name, and the sound is distant, as if coming from a long way off.

It has me frowning because this isn't part of the nightmare. There's never anyone in it but me. No one alive, that is.

Shaking my head because I know I must be hearing things, I turn my attention back to the door I'm desperate not to open. Slowly, I turn the handle and brace myself for what I'll find.

That's when I hear my name again, sounding a little louder this time, but not loud enough, not distinct enough for me to make out who it is.

It's vaguely familiar, and I pause for a second as I try to work out where I've heard it before.

Then I hear it again, only this time it's right against my ear. So close I feel the brush of lips against the shell of my ear. *"Savannah."* At the same time, a heavy hand presses down on my shoulder, the same shoulder I told Jeremy never to grab.

My reaction is instinctive.

I spin from the door and punch. Hard.

Bone crunches.

An unexpected pain in my hand shocks me, and then I'm blinking as I struggle to understand where I am, why my hand hurts, and why I'm in a room so devoid of light that I can't see a thing.

"Fuck. I think you broke my nose."

Oh.

Right.

The voice in my dream.

"Jeremy?" I whisper, even though I know it can't be him. It just doesn't feel like him.

"No. Jackson. His brother."

I start asking about Jeremy, then I stop. "Jeremy has a brother? Why didn't he tell me?"

"How about we go ask him? Come on, let's go."

I feel the disturbance of air in front of my face as he moves, likely rising to his feet. Not that I see a damn thing.

"Here, grab my hand."

I slap his hand back. "Hey! Watch it. Only two people get to put their hand where you just had it and you aren't one of them."

There's a moment of silence, then a choked laugh. "Uh, sorry about that."

I can feel his embarrassment, which makes it easier to forgive him.

Since I have a better idea about where Jackson is now, I raise my hand toward him. But then a thought occurs to me, and I draw my hand back. "I'm not in danger of putting my hand… you know… somewhere… private, am I?"

"How should I know?" Jackson asks, sounding like he's shrugging.

I stare at where he must be standing or crouching since his voice is coming from slightly above me. "You're both perverts. Aren't you?"

"Probably. Come on, we don't have long to get you out of here."

I reach out and thankfully grab hold of what feels like his thigh instead of something likely to get me into trouble with Jeremy. It's big. A lot bigger than I was expecting.

Jackson promptly takes my hand and places it on an equally muscled arm.

"Wow, you must seriously work out," I murmur, as I slowly get to my feet and follow his confident steps across the basement.

"You thinking you've ended up with the wrong brother?"

"You're both Stones," I whisper back. "I doubt there's a right one."

"Mmm, lucky Jeremy," he says. "Careful, there are stairs. Just take them one at a time."

With Jackson walking ahead of me up the stairs, it's easy for me to tell where the next one is and I follow along, one step at a time.

When we reach the top, Jackson pauses for a second, and I get the sense he's listening with his head cocked, even if I can't see him doing it.

He moves forward a step, and I follow with my hand wrapped around as much of his left arm as I can.

I shut my eyes to a sliver to protect them from the light after being near blinded the last time, but when we step into a dingy and dark hallway, I realize the hallway isn't just dark because there are no lights on, but because it's night-time.

How long was I in the basement?

In front of me is a hulking guy who is… *built*. Like, hits the gym every single day of the week, even on a Sunday level of built.

And I punched him in the face. Wow.

Without a word, Jeremy leads the way to a door at the end of the hallway, and we step out onto the Merrick house porch.

We creep down the front stairs, and then we're sprinting across the clearing and darting into the forest. I count my lucky blessings that other than a mild discomfort in my belly, sleeping seems to have helped work out the sickness caused by the tranq dart from my system, so I easily keep up with Jackson.

For several minutes I follow Jackson, wanting to know where he's taking me, but not knowing if we need to stay silent until we're further away from the house.

Finally, Jackson slows to a walk and then stops before he drops my hand and deliberately steps away from me.

As I'm turning to ask him why we've stopped, I'm grabbed and hauled against an overly warm body before lips find mine. Instantly, I know who it is.

Jeremy.

I wrap my arms and legs around him and kiss him back.

He backs us against a tree and tangles his hands in my hair. I moan into his mouth as our kiss turns frantic, and then I grab at the hem of his shirt because I need him right now.

"Uh, yeah. Guys, maybe hold off on the tender loving for a second."

The voice, so like Jeremy's, reminds me we're not alone.

Only Jeremy doesn't seem to care.

He continues to kiss me with a thoroughness that has me wishing Jackson would go far, far away, for another minute before breaking away to gaze up at me with a smile in his eyes. "Hey, sweet."

I know I'm wearing a stupid smile as I stare down at him with my arms wrapped around his shoulders. I'm so relieved to see him it's unreal. "Hey," I murmur.

And then we just stand there, staring at each other.

Jackson clears his throat. "Yeah, well. We need to move. You find that other shifter, Jer?"

My smile falls away at Jackson's words, and I turn to him before freezing.

Wow.

He's like a seriously hot, built, shaggy-haired version of Jeremy.

"What do you mean, hot version?" Jeremy snarls.

Which is when I realize I've been thinking out loud.

Oops.

"And close your mouth."

I snap my gaping mouth shut and turn away from

the smirking man-beast Jackson to a glowering Jeremy. "I just meant he was hot. You *know* I think you're hot."

Jeremy narrows his eyes as if he doesn't believe me. Then his expression shifts, and he starts looking a lot less angry.

I glare at him. "No. I am not about to do whatever nasty fantasy popped into your head to prove it."

The glower returns, and Jackson barks out a laugh. "Oh, I like her, Jer. I really do."

To my relief, Jeremy aims his ire at Jackson next. "Shut up. And what happened to your nose? You're bleeding."

"Your mate, that's what," Jackson grumbles.

Jeremy turns back to me, except this time he doesn't look pissed. His eyes are creased with concern. "You had a nightmare."

I blink at him in surprise. "How did you know?"

"Maybe because you damn near took my head off when I tried to wake you before."

At the mention of my nightmares, especially in front of a stranger, even if it is Jeremy's brother, I wriggle and look away. "How about putting me down now?"

Jeremy holds onto me tighter and tugs my head back to him, so we're eye to eye. "You okay?"

"It's no big deal. I'm fine. And when were you planning on telling me you had a brother?" I demand as I shove at his chest to remind him to put me down sometime this century.

Reluctantly, Jeremy lowers me on my feet, though the glower is back, and I don't understand why until he speaks.

"Tonight. I was going to introduce you to the new alpha of Dawley tonight. Only I get back to the hotel for the front desk to tell me they saw my mate leaving with a bag. A bulging one, they said. Running away, in other words. Luckily someone found your bag outside and it was easy to work out something must've happened to you."

I guess I have some explaining to do.

Then the rest of his words hit me. "What do you mean, the new alpha of Dawley?"

Jackson's sigh is full of frustration. "Seriously, have you two had a single conversation? Do you just fuck and argue all day?"

I stare at Jeremy, and he stares back. We turn to Jackson.

"So, what's the plan?" we ask him in unison.

Which turns out to be exactly the wrong thing to say, because suddenly Jeremy and Jackson are glaring at me, and I know they're about to tell me it isn't safe.

"I'm coming," I say, cutting them off before they can say a word.

Although Jackson has a fierce glower on his face, one that matches Jeremy's almost exactly, Jeremy grabs hold of my arm and tugs me away.

"Come on, we need to talk."

"I don't see why you're leading me away. It's not like Jackson won't hear," I mutter.

Jackson's low voice follows us. "She has you there, Jer."

"Fuck off, Jackson," Jeremy says without any heat, in the tone of someone who's said the same thing more times than they could count.

"He's older, isn't he?" I ask Jeremy.

"Yeah, by five years. Was it the wrinkles that gave him away?" Jeremy asks, his lips curving into a grin when Jackson's curse follows us.

"No, just wondered." I go back to wondering as Jeremy leads us further away from Jackson. If Jackson is five years older, that puts him in his early thirties, which is kind of unusual since we shifters mate younger than that, especially alphas.

"Jeremy, why doesn't Jackson have a mate?"

Jeremy halts and swings to face me. "This isn't you volunteering, is it? Because you remember you're taken, right?"

Even though it's night, and we're in a dark forest, I see enough of his expression to guess what he's saying.

I step into his body, sliding my arms around his shoulders before I rise onto my tiptoes and kiss him. In response, Jeremy smooths his hands down my back and grips my ass, grinding his cock against me with a low groan.

Although I don't say a word, I tell him with my kiss that I have a mate, and it's not Jackson.

When Jeremy breaks the kiss and gazes down into my face, he's smiling.

It's a new smile, soft and warm, and one I don't know how to respond to, so I take my hands off him and step back. "I think we're far enough away for you to say what you want to, so I can tell you it's not going to change my mind about going with you, and then we can go back to Jackson."

My words wipe the smile off his face.

When Jeremy presses my back against a tree with a heavy sigh, I guess this isn't going to be the angry tongue lashing I was expecting.

"Savannah, this won't be the same as the Blackshaw fight against the Merrick pack," he starts.

I blink at him in confusion because he shouldn't know anything about that fight unless he's been talking with Dayne. "Jeremy?"

Jeremy shakes his head. "Another time. We'll talk, I promise."

From somewhere behind us, I hear Jackson snort. Jeremy and I ignore it.

"Look, Jackson's slipped into this would-be pack and there are some seriously nasty shifters here."

I think of Loren and Maria and frown. Maria, I didn't trust, but she's a submissive wolf, and although Loren was a bitch, I wouldn't describe her as seriously nasty. The guy who stabbed me, maybe. "But—"

Jeremy shakes his head. "You wouldn't have seen most of them. Jackson has. There's more, and they're coming to the house, tonight. Presumably, they wanted to have some fun with you before they started cutting pieces off you."

His eyes are dark and there's a growl in his voice that tells me how much he's holding back.

"So, they'll be looking for me, then. Specifically." My mouth goes dry at the thought of the guy from the hotel. The one who stabbed me.

"Loren said there was a shifter called Chris who was going to be doing it. Cutting pieces off me." As soon as I say the words, I wish I didn't when Jeremy's eyes turn wolf, and his fingers grip me tighter.

"No one is going to be—"

I lean into him. "I know. But how many are we expecting?"

"Six. Maybe seven. There might be more," Jackson says, emerging from the forest. "It's clear they don't trust me. Jer and I planned on dealing with some of them earlier, but none of them were where they told me they'd be. They probably think I'm interested in the top job once we get rid of the new would-be alpha of Dawley and his mate."

I stare at Jackson as I try to process his words before turning to Jeremy.

"It was all a set-up. You wanted them—you wanted all of them to think you and I were going to lead so Jackson could join their ranks."

He nods. "Yes. What we have here is a mix of some

of the nastiest shifters in the country, Savannah. Some have reputations so bad, even *I* don't want to be anywhere near them."

I think back to grinning Stabby McStabberson back at the hotel and I get the message.

"Savannah?"

I turn to Jackson, and at the apology in his hazel eyes, I shake my head. "Don't you dare apologize for that."

He nudges Jeremy aside, and to my surprise, Jeremy doesn't tell him to fuck off, which makes me think they talked about this before.

Jackson steps closer and places a large hand at the back of my head before leaning in close, sending his shaggy, shoulder-length hair spilling forward. "I was tailing him. I should've seen what he would do, and instead, I was slow. I have plenty to apologize for."

I reach up and cover his hand with mine. "You saved me. That's what matters."

Jackson flashes a quick grin and bends to press a kiss to my brow. "I think we'll have to disagree about that, but thanks," he says, and releases me before retreating.

For a second, I think about all the danger I'll be putting myself into, and even though the idea of seeing Chris sends alarm shooting through me, I know can't walk away.

Going back to the hotel and sitting on my thumbs

feels wrong on so many levels that I can't see myself doing it. Maybe it's the alpha part of me, or maybe it's something else, I don't know.

I might be face to face with shifters like Owen. Like Abel. Something in Jeremy's eyes warns me this is a real possibility.

He's trying to protect me from more of the nightmares, more of the ghosts.

I suck in a deep breath before releasing it, then I step out of my boots and reach for my shirt.

"Savannah, what are you doing?" Jeremy asks.

"Getting ready to shift." I pull my shirt over my head.

"Savannah."

I lift my head and meet Jeremy's eyes. "These shifters are dangerous. If we don't stop them, they *will* hurt someone else, and I refuse to let that happen. So, I'm going to shift, and so are you and Jackson, and we're going to put a stop to all of this, once and for all."

Jeremy stares into my eyes for a long moment, then he hauls me close for a brief hard kiss before he reaches for his shirt.

I unbutton my jeans, start tugging them down my legs.

"Jackson, will you take your fucking eyes off my mate," Jeremy snarls, making me jump.

I turn to find Jackson eyeing me, and I smile brightly at him. "Sorry, I'm Jeremy's, you'll have to get your own."

Jackson's bark of surprised laughter has a smile spreading across my face as he turns his back. "Sure thing, darlin'. Sure thing."

CHAPTER TWENTY

Nothing could've prepared me for the fury of the big gray wolf, who moments ago was pacing quietly beside me, exploding out of the forest.

Jackson doesn't give the ten or more wolves in front of the Merrick house a chance to retreat, to fight back, to do anything but die under his powerful jaws. And Jeremy? He's no lightweight either.

But me? I freeze, stunned by their speed and their violence.

On the edge of the front porch is Loren and another shifter, who I'm guessing is another Merrick because they're the only ones who haven't shifted. In their hands are rifles, and it takes no stretch of the imagination for me to guess what they've loaded the guns with.

Tranquilizer darts.

They not only knew we were coming, but they'd prepared for us.

Looks like Jackson was right about them not trusting him.

All I can do is stare as they fire dart after dart at Jackson and Jeremy, and the Stone brothers just... keep on fighting as if they're being bothered by flies.

Loren's face twists in disgust before she flings her rifle away and stalks inside.

That's the thing with tranquilizer darts. It's hit and miss. Although it's more likely to work on us in our wolf shape, there's no guarantee it'll work at all. And when it does work, it's hard to know how it'll affect us.

Sickness is a known side effect, but there are other, more serious ones, like a sudden heart attack.

Luckily, I seem to have got away with a milder reaction than some, and most definitely than Talis. Maybe it's because Loren hadn't dosed me up to the extent Glynn Merrick did to her, or maybe my body just handles it better, I can't say.

As far as I can tell, the darts don't seem to have any effect on Jackson and Jeremy, and it looks like Loren's plan to end the fight with a rifle from a nice safe place has just gone out the window.

She should've learned from Glynn Merrick that there's no such thing as an easy win. Not when you're dealing with shifters. If she wants the Stone brothers dead, it looks like she's going to have to get her hands dirty.

Now, with the rifles rendered useless, the other shifter tosses his gun aside and shrugs out of his shirt to shift, and that's my sign to join the fray.

How Jeremy and Jackson knew about the Merrick packs fondness for tranquilizer darts is another mystery Jeremy hasn't revealed, but, before we shifted, they made me promise to stay back until they were out of play.

While I'd like to think that Jackson saw the rifles or one of the shifters let on they had them, I have a feeling they knew about the rifles in the same way they knew about our fight with the Merrick pack. Namely, that they've been in Dawley much longer than a few days or weeks. That or they've been speaking with Dayne.

Even though I know I should've joined the fight by now, I don't move, because I'm realizing that Jeremy was right. My being here wasn't a good idea. At all.

I'm in way over my head.

This is… too much. Way too much.

The blood, the death, the snarls, the pain, all overwhelm me.

In my wolf shape, I back up a step.

Jackson uses his larger body to force a snarling gray-brown wolf to the ground before he lowers his head and tears out his throat.

My heart labors as I stare at the pool of blood forming under the dead shifter, and I think of all the blood under Angel's door.

From several feet away, a wolf snarls. It's a sound

that's familiar to me, even though it's one I've only heard coming from a man's mouth.

I jerk my head to the side and see Jeremy, a less hulking version of Jackson with hazel eyes, standing over the body of a dead wolf, eyes fixed on mine, and there's a question in his eyes.

He wants to know if I'm okay.

A wolf takes advantage of his distraction and lunges at him. When they go down, my eyes are drawn back to the blood.

In it, I see my nightmares. I see death. I feel something evil, and I know it's coming for me.

That's when I hear him. Owen.

He's found where I've been hiding.

Blood, still fresh, covers his face and that's all I can focus on as he crouches in front of me with a smile I don't trust. "Time to shift now, Savannah. Angel couldn't be what I needed, but you can. But first I need you to shift."

Even though it's the last thing I want—the absolute last thing—he's my alpha, and I'm afraid. So, I nod, and I shift.

An enraged growl drags me from my memories, and I blink at the sight of Jackson fighting off three wolves at once. But that's not all that's happening in front of me.

Jeremy takes a wolf down and shoots me a look loaded with meaning.

And then I realize what I've done.

In the middle of a fight, I've shifted to human, and Jeremy isn't the only one who's noticed.

Two wolves turn away from Jeremy and toward me, their mouths gaping open in a wolfy grin. But their eyes…

I see the darkness in their eyes, and that's when I know what Jeremy was telling me to do.

Run.

I sprint through the forest, dodging trees, running as if my life depends on it, because right now? You can bet your ass that it does.

All I need is two minutes. Two minutes to calm my frantic heartbeat, and to silence my fear long enough to shift back.

I need to buy myself some time.

On the heels of my thought, a solid weight hits me in the back and I go down, cracking my head on the ground hard enough to stun me.

But just as I'm preparing to meet my maker, the weight is suddenly gone, and I hear the vicious growls of a fight happening somewhere behind me.

Jeremy.

He came after me.

As I'm getting my feet under me, someone grabs my hair and jerks me forward.

I cry out and reach up to tear the hands free, but the grip is merciless.

Never have I hated having long hair so fucking much as I do this minute, so much so, I have serious thoughts about cutting it off if I manage to survive this.

But right now, I'm blinded by my own hair, and whoever has hold of me is strong enough to make the grip unbreakable.

He drags me across the forest floor and away from Jeremy, who sounds like he's in a fight against more than just the wolf who tackled me.

Which means I'm on my own.

I don't beg for my life or scream or cry because I can see two ways this is going to go, and both versions end up with me dead.

Finally, when he's dragged me a few feet away, he stops and flings me so hard against a tree that the blow makes everything go black.

I lay in a crumpled heap at the base of the tree as I try to stop myself from passing out.

Now is not *the time to be helpless and unconscious, Savannah.*

"You with me yet?" The male voice is distant as if I'm at a bottom of a well. One that echoes.

I shake my head to focus on it, but I keep wanting to close my eyes.

A harsh voice penetrates my daze at the same moment I feel something poking me in the same place the shifter stabbed me. Right under my rib.

"Not even a scar. I can't say I'm not a little disappointed. I'd hoped to leave you with something to remember me by."

My alarm turns into icy dread because I know who this shifter is.

I remember his smile as he stabbed me in the hotel foyer.

I struggle to get up.

The shifter grabs a handful of my hair and smashes my head against the tree. Hard. I slump back to the ground with a moan of pain.

And then, randomly, I remember… Jeremy.

A vision flashes in front of my eyes.

It's Jeremy, holding me in his arms, his lips pressed against my brow as I moan in pain. He grabs a towel and presses it to my chest, only seconds later it's soaked with blood, and he replaces it with another, and then another.

Why would I be thinking about Jeremy now?

The shifter is speaking, but his words are merging with Jeremy's and it's hard to focus on one.

"Baby, I need you to wake up. I need you to be okay," Jeremy is saying.

I turn to his voice because I don't want to hear what this shifter with the cold eyes plans to do with me. He's like Abel. Like Owen. A predator.

Instead, I turn to Jeremy's voice.

"I fell in love with you the moment you walked into the bar."

I go still at hearing his murmur against my hair.

He said he told me about all the things he'd do to the shifter who stabbed me, not that he loved me.

"You were this vision from my dream. This mass of sunlight hair, those big stormy blue eyes filled with shadows. You didn't belong there. You didn't belong anywhere near someone like me. But somehow, you were mine."

Someone like him?

"I knew I wouldn't let you go. I knew I'd do everything I could to keep you. And when you said all you wanted was a one-night stand, I knew that was impossible because you belonged with me. Forever."

I grunt at a sharp pain in my side. I guess the shifter wants to have a bit of fun with me before he puts me out of my misery.

"You left before I could tell you how I felt. Before I could show you that you were already in my heart, and I was already in yours, from that first night."

Jeremy's words don't make any sense, and I fight to remember that first night in his apartment as another kick leaves me gasping in agony.

That first night.

The first night we fell asleep wrapped in each other's arms, so close there wasn't a bit of space between us. We breathed the same air. We were… a perfect fit. Meant to be.

A flutter deep inside me makes me catch my breath. *Mate.*

Our mate bond was forming—*had* formed even before he bit me. He was my mate. Right from the start.

My fated mate.

Impossible.

It's so rare, it almost never happens. I don't know anyone with a fated mate. I don't know anyone who even *knows* anyone with a fated mate.

Only now I do. Me and Jeremy.

The blows keep coming, but I don't feel them anymore.

I reach for Jeremy because he should be there, inside my heart, in that place reserved for your mate. And I find him. Right there, buried among all my pain, all my guilt, all the darkest parts of me, where I try never to look.

But all those places are in my heart. Right where the piece of Jeremy lives. I see his light, his love, his... bond with me.

I know it's always been there. No, not know, I *feel* it.

He's always been there, but I never thought to look.

No wonder he always knew me. No wonder he could always tell when I was holding things back.

"No, sweet. That's not the bond. I just know you. *Now, before you kill me. Use some of that strength you reserve for fighting me and put this guy out of his misery."*

I still at the sound of Jeremy's voice. Except this is no memory, but him. Right here, with me.

Mentally, I shake my head. He's wrong about me, and I try to tell him.

"I don't have any strength, I don't have—"

Jeremy shoves so many memories at me, I struggle to see them all at once.

He shows me all the times I refused to back down, all the times I argued back, all the times I stared him down, shoved back, broke Jackson's nose, refused to give in, came to Dawley to rescue Talis, stayed to fight because stopping these shifters was important. So important, I was willing to risk my life to do it.

He shows me more strength than I thought I had.

"There's more. But I wouldn't want you getting a big head. Now get up, sweet. And fight." Jeremy's voice is tinged with amusement, but anger too.

He knows what the shifter's doing to me, and I'm just lying here and taking it.

Anger stirs.

No. This isn't anger stirring, this is rage.

There's an ocean of it reserved for people like him. People like this shifter. Predators who think they can do whatever they want—hurt whomever they want—and be able to get up and walk away. They leave behind a trail of devastation. Broken people. Shattered hearts.

Dayne put three down, and it's about time I did the same.

"Hey!" I choke out.

The shifter stops kicking me, and I feel him move closer.

I open my eyes and find him crouched in front of me, excitement stirring in the dark depths of his gaze.

"Have you decided to fight? I hoped you would. It always makes things more interesting. I'll give you a minute to get up if you want or—"

My hand lashes out and locks tight around his throat. I squeeze and he chokes. And then I shove with all my rage, all my fury.

I am *not* weak, and I am *not* something for him to toy with. I might not have been strong enough to stop Owen, but I can stop this guy. No problem.

The shifter goes flying.

I get to my feet, ignoring all my aches and all my pains, never taking my eyes off him.

He slowly sits up with a smile of anticipation on his face, and my vision changes as my wolf studies him with disgust, mired with fury.

No mercy.

My wolf and I are in perfect agreement.

I launch myself at him, forcing myself into the fastest change of my life.

Only an alpha can shift on the move in seconds, and this guy made a big mistake staying human. A mistake that's going to cost him his life, because he's no alpha.

I see the moment of realization dawning in his eyes as he scrambles back, his hand going to protect his throat.

A second later, I'm landing on him as a wolf and I'm tearing out his throat.

"Well, I'll be. Pretty, and deadly. I do like her, Jer."

I turn from the dead shifter beneath my jaws to find Jackson leaning against a tree, his arms folded over his chest.

But he isn't my focus. Jeremy, still in his wolf shape,

looking as if he were rushing to get to the shifter, only I beat him to it, is.

I watch him shift, quickly, easily, not as fast as my shift but fast all the same.

Once he's human, it's my turn, and I take a second to wipe the dead shifter's blood from my face. Since I can't do anything about the taste of his blood in my mouth, I don't bother.

"Hey, sweet," Jeremy says, his eyes unreadable.

"Hey."

We regard each other in silence.

"That was some shift," he says.

I see it so clearly in his eyes then, the knowledge that he's mine, that he's my fated mate, and I don't know how I missed it all this time.

"You're an ass," I snap.

He blinks at me.

Jackson snorts. "Yep."

"What did I do to deserve that?" Jeremy asks.

"For not telling me. That's what. You're the biggest ass in the world because—" My eyes fill with tears, and his expression turns to horror as he rushes over to me.

"Hey, don't cry. I didn't mean to make you cry." He gathers me in his arms and spins me so I've got my back to Jackson.

"Stop shooting panicked glances at Jackson. I'm not acting hysterical," I snarl against his chest.

Jackson laughs, and I hear him walking away. "I'll leave you to it, brother."

I pull away so I can glare at Jeremy. "Why didn't you tell me? I never would've left if you'd just… told me." I can't hold the tears back and they start flowing again.

Jeremy folds me into his arms and presses his lips against my hair. "I'm sorry, sweet."

"You'd better be." I burrow my face against his neck. "And, we need to talk to each other, because Jeremy, we *need* to talk."

Jeremy presses his lips against my brow. "We will."

"And I'll kill you if you hide something that big from me again."

"I know."

"I'm being serious. I will. I'll toss you from the balcony or I'll drown you in the bath."

He eases back and tilts my head up to his. "I know you will." His eyes are smiling.

"And I love you."

The smile in his eyes touches his lips, and he bends them to mine. "I know that too."

"And do you—"

"Sweet, don't even think about asking me such a stupid question. I know you're a model but—"

I grab his hair and pull his face down. Because I have to kiss him. No, because I *need* to.

Jeremy wraps his arms around me and kisses me back.

It's heaven, or it would be if we weren't both covered in blood and sharing a space with a dead body. But otherwise, it's perfect.

CHAPTER TWENTY-ONE

"How did Paulo handle the news you were quitting?"

I continue to stare down at the early morning traffic from the balcony of our hotel room.

After all the drama from last night's fight at the Merrick house, followed by my late-night call to Paulo after Jeremy and I got back to the hotel, I didn't expect to be in another one of Jeremy's shirts and on the balcony at four.

Jeremy fell asleep not long after we showered and made love, and once he had, something compelled me to stumble out of bed and go looking for my phone. I found it in my bag beside the front door, where he must have left it, and then I crawled back into bed.

Although Jeremy woke at the start of my conversation, he was asleep again by the end, and I realized, as I watched him sleep while talking with Paulo, that he hadn't been getting much sleep because of me.

"Surprisingly okay," I admit. "I sent him a picture of you naked. I think it helped him understand why I wouldn't—"

I shriek when Jeremy throws me over his shoulder and starts inside.

"Jeremy, put me down. I swear—"

He gives my ass a hard slap and I suck in a breath.

But when he follows it up with a firm rub, I only just manage to hide my moan. "I told you not to do that," I say, fighting to sound outraged.

Jeremy tosses me onto the bed and follows me down a second later. "Yeah, that's not going to work, sweet. I know exactly what that does to you," he says, gruffly.

He presses a kiss on my lips. "Exactly."

Does that mean he knows...?

"Yes. It does," he says. "And if you behave, I might do it again."

I stare at him for a moment, oddly excited by the prospect, then horrified at myself for liking it. "Uh, get off me. I'm disgusted with myself."

Jeremy doesn't move. "You want me to share some of my fantasies? Might make you feel less disgusted with yourself."

I snort. "And disgusted with you instead? No thanks."

We lay there in silence for a moment, Jeremy

running a hand distractedly through my hair. "You didn't really send him a picture of me naked, did you?"

I pat him on his shoulder and close my eyes. "Of course, I did. He had to know what was keeping me from taking the job. It was full frontal. Had to be. Paulo wouldn't have understood otherwise."

At Jeremy's continued silence, I open my eyes a peek and find him gazing down at me blankly. "What?"

"You really did, didn't you?"

"Yep." I close my eyes and go back to stroking his bare shoulder as Jeremy lays braced over me.

We lay in silence for a long time, and as the minutes tick by, I feel him studying me. And the longer it goes on without him saying a word, the more it disturbs my calm.

Yesterday, after Jackson caught me and Jeremy sneaking into the forest after our fight, he snapped at us to deal with the dead bodies first.

So, we spent the next several hours burying bodies. Amongst them was Maria.

I'd assumed it was Jackson who'd killed her, but when I asked him, he told me he thought it must've been Loren since he found her inside the house beside a packed bag. He guessed Maria had been about to run, and Loren had killed her to stop her, maybe believing that Maria had betrayed her.

While I had no love for Maria, I can't help but pity her for her life ending like that. The sad thing is if she'd gotten away from Loren and Glynn Merrick years ago, she would've survived, but fear kept her trapped with the Merrick's, and it ended up costing her life.

It's kind of ironic that Jackson admitted killing Loren when he caught her slinking away, so I guess that was instant karma.

Given how she'd been shooting tranquilizer darts at Jeremy and Jackson and was pretty much responsible for this whole revenge plot, there was no way Jackson was about to let her live another day only so she could disappear and come back to repeat it all a few months down the line.

No. She had to die.

Jeremy's fingers smooth hair from my face. "Savannah."

He says nothing but my name, but it's enough to make me tense, to have panic rising because I know what's coming.

"Savannah." This time, he presses a soft kiss to my lips, and I open my eyes.

He's trying to peer into my heart, into the darkness, and the shadowed places I never want anyone to see. Even I don't want to see them.

I shove him. Hard.

I send him flying out of bed and to the floor with a loud thud. The only reason it works is because he isn't expecting it.

I don't wait to see where he ends up. I'm too busy ripping my shirt off and then I leap from the bed, and by the time my feet touch the floor, I'm a wolf.

"Savannah!" My name is a snarl on Jeremy's lips, and I turn to find him crouched, closer than I would like, and his eyes have gone wolf.

Yeah, probably not the best thing I could have done.

But he's going to want to talk, and as a wolf, I can't. He'll have to catch me, pin me, and convince me to shift, and that's not going to happen.

I turn to stalk away.

"This isn't about me forcing you to talk, sweet."

His voice makes me pause, but I don't turn around.

"This is about you choosing to let me in. By choice. Because it's important you choose."

I turn and snarl at him.

Choice? What choice?

Anger surges at his words. The *universe* didn't give me a choice about which mate I'd have. *He* didn't give me a choice before he bit me. All of this just happened to me. And as much as I know I'm lucky to have found my soul mate when few ever do, a small part of me feels trapped by it.

To my surprise, Jeremy lies on the ground and stares up at the ceiling.

I stare at him, confused since I was expecting a full-blown wrestling match.

"I didn't think you'd have stayed, even if I'd told you. I knew you didn't want a mate. I could feel it. That's why I didn't tell you."

The quiet seriousness of his words holds me still before something compels me to pad closer.

Sensing this might be a trick, I halt far enough away from Jeremy that he can't grab me, and lay on the floor, my chin resting on my front paws.

"Come closer, sweet. I'd like to pet you."

I narrow my eyes in suspicion. Yet when he turns his head to me, there's no smirk, no smile in his eyes. He's perfectly serious, and that's what convinces me this is no trap, no trick.

I rise and move closer, close enough for him to bury his hands in my fur.

"Even as a wolf, you're beautiful. Soft golden fur. Pretty tail."

At his attempt to grab my tail, I growl, but it's playful rather than aggressive.

Pervert.

"Hey, it's not my fault my wolf likes your tail," Jeremy says, a smile touching his lips.

He closes his eyes and goes back to stroking my fur as I sink beside him and try not to purr. We wolves don't purr but my God, do I want to at the firm but insistent pressure of his hand stroking me in all the right places.

"You're a famous model. Jackson and I are lone wolves who never fit in anywhere, and had to work for every last bit of what we have. I didn't even have a pack to offer you, so I thought if I gave you the best sex of your life, you'd want to stay."

I snort.

Typical guy.

"Yeah," Jeremy admits with a sigh. "I know."

We fall back into silence.

"It's happened before, you know. A fated mate rejection."

I go still at his words.

What?

I feel the desperate need to shift so I can ask Jeremy, because what he's saying sounds impossible.

"I won't tell you why, but maybe one day he will."

Which means I know who it is, and since the only one connected to me and Jeremy is...

Jackson?

Jeremy lets out a tired sigh. "Don't push, sweet. Not my story to tell."

No, something like that wouldn't be. I feel like I know too much already. I can feel Jeremy's pain for his brother, and what would've devastated Jackson.

I couldn't imagine the other half of my soul rejecting me. And then it hits me: I nearly did the same to Jeremy.

God, no wonder he was so pissed.

I move closer, and when I do, Jeremy turns his head. He gazes at me without expression for several seconds.

And then I lower my head and lick his face.

When I pull my head back, he's staring at me like he can't believe I did it.

"Savannah, what was that?" Jeremy's voice is calm. Controlled. Yet his body trembles with the force of him trying to hold back his laughter.

I back up until his hand falls away from me, and then I shift to human.

I drop to the carpeted floor beside him, resting my head against his shoulder. "Wolf kiss," I tell him, curving my arm around his waist.

"You licked my eye. Half my face is wet." He lifts his arm, presumably to wipe his face before lowering his hand to stroke my hair. "Next time shift before you kiss me. Less messy."

"It depends where I kiss you."

Jeremy stops stroking my hair. "We're not talking about that right now."

"Are you sure, because—"

Jeremy takes my hand from around his hip and places it over his cock. It's rock hard and I feel it throbbing.

"You feel that, sweet?" His voice is gruff.

I swallow, closing my hand around it. "Yeah."

He pulls my hand away and puts it back on his side. "So."

I wait for him to say more, but when he doesn't, I lift my head so I can peer into his face. "So…?"

"So." Jeremy presses my head back to his chest and resumes carding his fingers through my hair.

"You realize that makes no sense at all, right?"

"Of course, it does."

He sounds so sure of himself that I can't stop myself from smiling, and then I think of us leading a pack.

"It's a good thing Jackson's running the Dawley pack. We'd be terrible at it," I say.

"I wouldn't want to share you with anyone," Jeremy admits.

"We don't know how to talk to each other, let alone other people."

"We'd be off somewhere having sex with each other instead of actually leading."

"And I—" I stop because we're veering into dangerous territory, territory I had no intention of going.

Jeremy waits for me to speak. He doesn't push. He doesn't say my name, just waits.

"I would let my pack die instead of protecting them."

I wait for the condemnation. The blame. The horror at what just came out of my mouth, but Jeremy continues stroking his hand through my hair as if I didn't just admit to being responsible for my pack members' deaths.

"Now we've got the guilt out of the way, you want to tell me what happened?"

Although my first response is to shove Jeremy, to lash out at him, I don't because I know he doesn't say it to hurt me, but to provoke me. "You know, you could've said it a nicer way," I tell him, as I try to put off talking about the thing I've been avoiding for days, weeks, months. Years.

I feel Jeremy nod. "I could. But nice doesn't work with you."

I grip onto him. "I don't want to talk about it. Any of it. Not ever."

"And you don't have to. Not all of it. Not all at once. We can do a bit at a time, and then I'll let you have sex with me, and then we can do something else."

"Jeremy Stone, are you attempting to get me to talk with the promise of hot sex as payment for my secrets?"

"Of course, I am."

I lift my head from Jeremy's chest and eye him in silence.

He looks so relaxed, laying stretched out naked on the floor, his hair still tousled from sleep. Also, probably from my raking my hands through it when we had sex last night.

He's not the mate I would've chosen.

No, I'd have gone for someone who I could convince to do what I want. Someone who'd love me but wouldn't push me too hard to probe the places in my heart that hurt too much for me to want to look at.

He isn't the mate I would've chosen, but he's the one I needed, and I think the universe knew that.

I'm glad he's mine.

I don't know what Jeremy reads on my face that has his eyes warming, but he buries a hand in my hair and draws me down for a kiss. "I love you too, sweet."

I fake glare at him. "Actually, I was thinking you were an ass."

He smiles at me. "No, you weren't."

Since Jeremy sounds so confident, I know there's no point trying to deny it, so I sigh and lay my head back down on his chest. "No, I wasn't."

We lay there in silence, as Jeremy strokes a hand through my hair.

"I suppose you heard about Dayne being the cold-blooded alpha," I start, with my eyes fixed on a potted plant in the corner of the room.

"I heard. But now I've met him, I have strong reservations they were nothing but rumors."

"Some things were true. Not all of them." And then I stop because I don't want to talk about this. "I need to get up."

Jeremy's arm tightens around my waist. "No, you don't."

He's right. I don't want to be anywhere other than in Jeremy's arms.

"I only have vague memories of my parents—my biological parents—since they died when I was so young. It wasn't anything anyone could've done, just slick rain, the wrong tires, and a dangerous road."

Starting here is good, I think. Painful. But a different kind of pain, more manageable.

Jeremy doesn't comment on my time jump, only squeezes me to show he's listening.

"The Blackshaws—Dayne really—took me into

their hearts. And that's all I knew. From then on, I was Savannah Blackshaw with an older brother, Dayne, and two sisters, Bridget and Angel. Dayne damned near tortured me by making me watch cartoons with him. I learned to cry on demand so someone would come and save me since arguing with him never seemed to work."

"Master manipulator at work," Jeremy murmurs, "at how old?"

"Six," I admit, smiling. "Angel taught me."

But then my smile falls away at the thought of Angel. "I can't talk about her and Bridget yet. I can't talk about the kids. Not yet. Not all at once."

It hurts too much.

"We can talk about that another time. After you tell me why you were burying poop in a sandbox."

I suck in a sharp breath and raise my head to glare at him. "You *were* eavesdropping!"

He grins up at me unrepentantly. "I couldn't help it. It wasn't like your friend was trying to keep her voice down."

I lower my head back to his chest. "Regan. I will kill her."

"Tell me why you think it's your fault they died," Jeremy says, his voice soft, undemanding.

After a pause, I nod. "I knew something was wrong with him—with our old alpha, Owen. I saw it in his eyes." My voice ends in a whisper.

"What did you see?"

He must know, since I nearly told him when we

were in the rental next to the Dawley National Forest and I was talking about Abel. Back when some wolf, probably Loren, tried to scare me away from Dawley, and nearly succeeded. At least that's what Jeremy and Jackson think.

"Predator."

Jeremy doesn't respond, but I can feel him listening. I know he wants me to keep talking, to talk through my thoughts.

I sigh. "He wasn't like that before. At least I don't remember seeing it in his eyes when I was younger. He fell in love with Angel, and when he realized he was losing her, I think it broke something inside him."

Jeremy doesn't ask for details. He's always been the observant kind, far too observant for my liking.

I think he can guess a lot of what I'm not saying, or rather, what I'm choosing to leave out.

"By then, Bridget had moved back home. Dayne was out trying to track down Talis, and an agent had scouted me, so I was getting more and more bookings. Back then, none of us were staying in the pack house a lot. Owen wanted it that way. Mostly I stayed with Dayne's parents in their house in town."

"And no one else saw this side of Owen?"

"I think some of the pack suspected what might be happening. Maybe they talked to him, I don't know. But he's—he was—alpha, so other than killing him, I don't know what they could've done. I mean, how do you tell an alpha their job is to protect the pack, not hurt it when you know he could kill you for it?"

Jeremy is silent for a long moment. "But you did. You said something."

I go back to staring at the potted plant. "I said something."

"And then?"

"And then he killed them all."

"But not you?"

I close my eyes and say my next words in a whisper, "He thought I might make a better Luna than Angel had."

"I see," Jeremy says after a long silence.

And something in his tone of voice tells me that he does.

"I should've told Dayne, or Luka, or someone else."

"Savannah." Jeremy rolls us until I'm lying on the floor, and he's braced over me, peering into my eyes. "You always have a good reason for deciding one action over another. Tell me why you didn't tell Dayne or Luka."

My smile is bitter. "So, you can blame me for it?"

His expression doesn't change. "I'm not going to waste either of our time responding to that. Tell me."

I swallow and fix my gaze over Jeremy's shoulder, as I think about all those years ago. "I knew Dayne would fight Owen. Owen was an alpha in his prime and he was… obsessed with Angel. Dayne was distracted about finding Talis. Owen would've killed him."

"Tell me why you didn't tell Luka or any of the other pack members."

Tears fill my eyes and I blink them away. "Owen would've killed or kicked out any other pack member who tried to intervene. He wouldn't have hesitated to punish them."

"And?"

I blink more tears away, but even though I feel Jeremy's gaze on my face, I can't bear to meet his eyes. "I didn't think anyone would believe me." I close my eyes. "I didn't want to be kicked out. Not when I didn't really belong."

"Baby…"

I meet Jeremy's eyes. "My parents—my biological parents—they weren't pack. Not really. They'd moved to Hardin because they wanted a fresh start. When they died, I would've had nowhere to go if Dayne's parents hadn't taken me in. If Owen hadn't agreed."

"And who told you this? Who threatened to kick you out?"

I shift my gaze to Jeremy's ear. "Owen," I whisper.

Jeremy nods. "So, you didn't tell anyone you thought the alpha was unhinged for good reasons, and you thought you could deal with it yourself. But I know you're not reckless enough to think you can take on an alpha in his prime yourself, so I'm guessing you told someone."

How can he know me so well?

"I told Dayne's parents. I told Bridget. I tried to tell Angel, but she said she knew Owen, knew that he'd growl a bit, but with all of us there, he wouldn't do anything more than that."

"But that isn't what happened."

Although I'm staring at him, it isn't Jeremy's face I see, but the day when our alpha lost himself to a wild rage. "No. That isn't what happened."

"Sweet?"

Jeremy's fingers brush back the hair from my face.

"He tore into them like they were enemies. Like they weren't family. His eyes…" I stop because I need to breathe. "I ran. I hid, and then he was there, his hand on my shoulder."

I shake at the memory of his hand closing around my shoulder and when I turned, he was there, his face covered with blood, and I knew all of them must be dead for him to have come after me.

I remember the predatory gleam in his eyes, and I tremble harder.

"I hit him, and I ran again. I shifted so I could find somewhere to hide. There was blood everywhere."

"Sweet." There's a note in Jeremy's voice as if he's telling me to stop, only now that I've started, I can't.

"He found me. Told me to shift. I knew what would happen if I didn't. So, I shifted. And then he told me I would be a better Luna than Angel. Less of a disappointment."

"Baby, stop now."

I'm sobbing with no memory of having started crying, or when my cheeks got so wet. "I threw myself down the stairs trying to get away. He came down after, one slow step at a time, and I couldn't move. I couldn't do anything. But then Luka was at the door because he thought something might be wrong. He came with some of the others, and Owen took off into the forest. Luka saw all the blood, and he guessed what must've happened. He called Dayne to come back. And Dayne went into the forest and killed Owen."

"And you went to live in a cabin in the woods."

"But it didn't matter where I lived, or where I went, the nightmares followed me everywhere. I'll never escape them. They'll haunt me forever."

"No, sweet. Not forever," Jeremy says, pressing my face to his neck and holding me close as I dissolve into tears. "I won't let them. We'll fight them together."

CHAPTER TWENTY-TWO

"Jeremy, when you said you'd help me fight my nightmares, this isn't exactly what I thought you had in mind," I say, handing Jeremy the screwdriver he requested.

"I think it's helping," he says, studying the instructions for the Ikea dresser he's building. "I mean, what could be a better distraction from nightmares than tackling Ikea furniture."

He's not wrong there.

In the two weeks since I broke down and finally told Jeremy about Owen, we've been settling into an apartment in Dawley, a rental for now, while we figure out what we want to do.

Jeremy admitted that he'd packed up his apartment in Chicago and put everything in storage here weeks before, when he tracked me down.

Apparently, there are more blonde models called Savannah and more modelling agencies than I could ever imagine. Certainly, more than he'd ever thought. In the thousands he told me. After he had, the rest was easy, since the number of blonde models called Savannah who were shifters, numbered one.

Even though we're renting, he's not in a hurry to unpack, and I'm not rushing to pack up all my things in Hardin.

Neither of us wants to stick around Dawley forever, but for now, it's as good a place as any. And strangely enough, in those two weeks, I've only had three nightmares so bad I woke in tears.

After each one, Jeremy and I have sex and cuddle before he drags me up to go build some furniture.

I would tell him it's the sex that helps take my mind off my nightmares rather than figuring out which screw goes where, but I won't.

There's something about watching Jeremy build furniture while he's naked...

I'm supposed to be helping him, but mostly I just hand him things and try not to get caught staring at his ass.

I should tell him about my nightmares changing. Only, I don't know how.

It's the reason I told Regan and Talis that Jeremy and I wouldn't be coming to Hardin for a while, that there were things we needed to deal with first.

So, when I need to run from my ghosts, we climb in his car and make the drive to what is now the Dawley-Stone pack land and we run until I've left my ghosts far behind.

"Sweet?"

I turn around and find Jeremy standing in the doorway.

He's been there a while. While he knows I need space to go away and think sometimes, he will find me when I'm in danger of sinking too deep into my memories.

I straighten from the balcony edge and go to him.

I don't say a word, just slip my hand in his and lead him back to our bed, and we climb in so we're lying side by side.

"I'm not having the same nightmares," I tell him.

"I know, sweet."

Of course, he would.

Since I can't lay this close to Jeremy without touching him, or without him touching me, I lay my hand flat on the bed between us and he covers it with his much larger, warmer one.

"We have sex a lot," I tell him.

He blinks at me, and I fight to hide my smile at his confusion. "Uh, what?"

"It's only a matter of time before I get pregnant."

The confusion on his face smooths away.

"I mean, Talis was pregnant in two weeks, and I

think we must have had at least three times the amount of sex they did."

Now it's his turn to fight back a smile as he moves his hand to my hip. "I'm guessing this is going somewhere, sweet."

"What if we're terrible parents? I mean, neither of us wants the responsibility of leading a pack, and I'd say a baby is an even bigger responsibility, wouldn't you?"

For a long moment, Jeremy regards me in silence.

I think back to one of our first serious conversations about our future.

It was strange hearing an alpha say they didn't want to lead a pack. When he told me shortly before we moved into this apartment, I didn't know what to say.

I felt stupid for thinking all alphas would want to lead a pack when, as an alpha, it's never interested me. It seems ridiculous now to imagine I'd be the only one to think that way.

"Savannah, leading a pack requires a level of dedication, and patience that I don't possess. I've never been interested in it. But for Jackson, this need to nurture and build a pack of his own is part of his DNA."

I wait for Jeremy to get to the point because I'm sure he has one. He always does.

"But a baby? Come here." He rolls onto his back and tugs me toward him until I'm straddling him, then he slips my shirt over my head and tosses it to the floor.

His eyes go to my stomach, and he brushes my aside hair.

When he places a large hand over my lower belly, I feel a fluttering at the thought of being pregnant with Jeremy's child. "When I think of my child growing right here, I know I will do whatever it takes—be whatever is required to give it the best life I can. I can walk away from leading a pack without a second thought. That means nothing to me. But you? It would kill me to do the same to our child."

The intensity in his whiskey brown eyes makes it impossible for me to look away.

I swallow because it feels like there's something stuck in my throat.

"Is that why you dropped your coffee in Denny's?"

I'd almost forgotten about him making me drop my coffee when he called me maternal, and I consider lying, but Jeremy and I have come so far since then. It doesn't seem right to.

I nod.

"Savannah. When I think of how fiercely you guarded that last donut the other day, I have no doubt that you will—"

I poke him between the ribs, and he lets out a far louder growl than the act warrants.

"Fuck! Savannah, that *hurt!*"

"Then don't compare our future baby to a donut. And it didn't hurt. You're just being a baby."

Eventually, Jeremy stops rubbing at the spot I poked

him, and he raises his hand to curve it around my nape. "Anything else you want to tell me before we go back to building furniture?"

Since I was expecting his next words to be about sex, I blink in surprise.

But when I see his lips twitching, I narrow my eyes. "I bet you think you're hilarious, don't you?"

"I do." He presses on my nape, and I bend over him for a soft, lingering kiss.

I sigh into his mouth as he deepens it. But when his hands go to my hips, to shift me back and onto him, I break the kiss.

Jeremy's eyes flutter open. "What is it, sweet?"

"Nothing I want to say," I tell him, and I reach for him through our mate bond.

Now there are fewer shadows, and less pain, I reach for him more.

My heart isn't as filled with all the things I was looking to avoid, it's slowly filling with memories of him, of our love, and it shines so bright, it's easy to focus on that instead of everything I've lost.

"I love you, Jeremy Stone," I tell him because I'm not sure I've shown him enough in the mate bond.

He rolls us and cages me between his arms. "I've always seen it. I've always known," he says, lowering his mouth to mine. "And I love you too, Savannah Stone."

"Wait a second, we didn't talk about—"

Jeremy kisses me, and my complaint, my arguments, all of it fades into nothing.

I wrap my arms and legs around him, and we come together so perfectly as if we were made for each other.

And then I remember we were.

I smile against his lips.

Mate.

EPILOGUE

"I never thought I'd ever get so much pleasure seeing something being destroyed," I murmur against Jeremy's chest as he holds me against him.

"You and me both," Talis says, from a few feet away, rubbing her pregnant belly.

At five months, what was a gentle curve is now a full-on bump, and the level of Dayne's possessiveness as he stands guard over her makes me feel a touch sorry for her.

Then I remember what Jeremy is like and I know with utter certainty he'll be a million times worse when it's our turn.

"I know what you're thinking, you know," the object of my thoughts mutters darkly, "and I don't think I appreciate it."

I stand on my tiptoes to press a kiss on his lips. "But

I notice you didn't deny it," I say once I've pulled back.

Before he can respond, there's a sound of a truck pulling up, and I turn to see it's Jackson wearing a red and black checked shirt in a battered blue truck.

"I'll be right back," Jeremy says, giving me one last kiss before he goes to help Jackson with the beers and other barbeque food he picked up from the store for our late afternoon get-together.

Although we could've eaten back at the rental the Blackshaw pack has once again claimed as home for the weekend, we all wanted to be here to see Talis' old hellhole of a home go down.

Now that it lies in ruins with the destruction team gone not too long ago, it's time to rebuild and turn what was once a place filled with pain and darkness into something new.

Jackson is ready to get to work rebuilding a pack in Dawley, and that means starting with a home.

"So, Paris, huh?" Talis asks, turning her back on her old home to face me.

"Yeah, Paris," I say, watching the Stone brothers unload Jackson's truck.

"He's... uh. Kind of—" Talis stops, and I turn to see what stopped her.

Dayne glowering down at her proves to be it.

"Yeah." I sigh, torn between staring at the muscles straining beneath Jackson's shirt and checking out Jeremy's ass. "I know, right?"

"Savannah, don't encourage her," Dayne snaps

before shaking his head. "So, how long will you guys be gone?"

I shrug. "I don't know. I'd like to show Jeremy everywhere and go to all the places I never had a chance to."

"But being an airhead model got in the way, huh?" Regan says, slipping in beside me.

"I was never an airhead," I tell her. "But I get what you're trying to say. I don't know what I'll do next, but I've got savings, and Jeremy's promised to make sure I never run out of ramen, so I think I'll be okay."

"Well, it looks like between him and Jackson, everything is well in hand here," Dayne says, in a way that has me narrowing my eyes at him in suspicion.

"You knew," I guess.

"He told me a little about what they wanted to do, and I can't say I wasn't relieved to hear it. The Merrick situation needed dealing with, but there was no way I was going to leave Talis to clean it up."

I gape at him. "But you were only in your office for five, ten minutes, max."

"There wasn't a lot that needed to be said. Namely that he would take care of you, and deal with the situation here. Once I knew that my mind was at rest."

"Well, you might have said something to me about it," I grumble.

"But you're okay?" Dayne asks, his voice casual, but his eyes intense, probing.

I reach out and grab his arm because he's family and

I need to touch him. "Yeah, I think I will be," I tell him. And for the first time since he asked me years ago, after he killed Owen and came to find me, I mean it.

"Good." He wraps his arm around my shoulder in a hard hug before pulling away and ruffling my hair until I glare at him. He grins down at me, unrepentant.

Family.

It's going to be hard, being away from them all. Being so far away. But a late-night talk with Jeremy led to an argument about where we could get the best pastries. I insisted Paris, and he said New York, and he told me to prove it.

So, I said why not.

Since we don't have any plans for the future, we figure why not do some traveling first, and with us gone, Jackson can take over our apartment if he wants instead of staying in the big rental by the national forest.

"Anyhoo, who's muscles?" Regan asks, her eyes fixed on Jackson's ass as he finishes unloading the last of the cases of beer for our BBQ.

"Jackson," I say. "Jeremy's brother."

"Oh, he's..."

I never find out what Regan was going to say because she suddenly stops speaking.

I glance at Jackson to see what's caught her attention and find his eyes fixed in our direction.

Without a word to Jeremy, Jackson shoves the last crate of beer at him, forcing him to take it or drop it.

"Jackson, what the fuck?" Jeremy snarls.

But Jackson isn't paying the least bit of attention to his brother. He leaps from the top of his truck and then he's moving toward us. Fast.

I frown at the intensity in his eyes. "I wonder what—"

Only, like Regan, I never get to finish my sentence because I turn to discover she is no longer standing beside me.

No, Regan's sprinting off into the forest.

"Hey!" Jackson roars. "Come back here!"

We all stand around, mouths hanging half opened as Jackson tears off after Regan into the forest, wondering what the hell just happened.

To find out what has Regan running
You can find out in
IRON-HEARTED ALPHA
Now available to pre-order.

ALSO BY EVE BALE

Voracious Vampires of Las Vegas

The Lottery

Hellfire

Deepest Rage

Deepest Pain

Deepest Love

The Bladed

Hellfire

Deacon

Julian

Hunter (COMING SOON)

Cold-Blooded Alpha

Cold-Blooded Alpha

Hot-Blooded Alpha

Stone-Hearted Alpha

Iron-Hearted Alpha

THANK YOU

Thank you so much for you picking up Stone-Hearted Alpha.

If you'd like to never miss a new release, and pick up your subscriber exclusive story, you can keep updated by joining my mailing list here: www.evebale.com/newsletter

You can also "like" my Facebook page at: www.facebook.com/AuthorEveBale

As a new indie author, reviews mean a lot. So, if you enjoyed Stone-Hearted Alpha and would like to share that with other readers, it would mean the world to me if you'd leave a review.

XOXO

While we are talking about the big things, it's not easy. It doesn't come easy for either of us since I struggle to talk about what happened without wanting to run, and Jeremy is apt to keep things from me because he's never had to share his life with someone before.

And he has this weird hang-up that I'm better than him, and it's only a matter of time before I realize it and leave him. I can't help but think it has something to do with what happened with Jackson and a fear our relationship will end the same way.

With a sigh, I wander out of the lounge while Jeremy is distracted and head for the balcony. Although I miss our larger hotel room balcony, it's outside, and I still get a nice view of the dark streets below.

It's late. About midnight I think, but the streets are still pretty busy. I think it's the reason Jeremy wanted me to see this place, and every time I step out because I need to breathe, I want to cry because he knew what I needed, and he gave it to me without my having to ask for it.

He never pushes me to talk, and when I have a flashback or I want to run, he takes one look at me and he says we should go running, and we do.

With Jackson staying at the Merrick house since it and all the surrounding land now officially belongs to the Stone brothers who, I recently learned, did okay for themselves investing in property, we go there.

Printed in Great Britain
by Amazon